Beyond My Expectation

Flairs and Glairs
Publication House

Disclaimer

This is a work of fiction and solely represent the thoughts of the corresponding authors of the articles. Our editors have tried their best to edit the content of all the authors and check the plagiarism.

All the write-ups in this book are unique and are only published in this book.

In case any plagiarism or error is found, only the author is responsible alone, and not the publisher or the Compilers.

Cover Designing and Book Formatting
Shubham Shah and Ishani Agarwal

Acknowledgment

We put our wholehearted thanks to 'Flairs and Glairs Publication' to provide us this wonderful opportunity. Our heartfelt thanks to Mr. Shubham Shah(Founder), Ms. Ishani Agarwal(Co-founder), and Ms. Sahina Ghugha (Project Head) for their co -operation and e ncouragement at every point of obstacle that we faced.

We appreciate and cherished all our Co-authors who have put their soul and heart to our anthology 'Beyond My Expectation' and showed their talent through their constructive ideas and to keep positive   attitude towards us. We blessed you all that you accomplish your goals in your life.

We really obliged to the whole team who become part of this Anthology "Beyond My Expectation"and cooperated with us at every phase to make this dream project successful.

Co-Authors

Shubham Shah (Founder Flairs and Glairs)
Ishani Agarwal (Co-Founder Flairs and Glairs)
Sahina Ghugha (Project Head)
Neha Gupta (Compiler)
Riya Mandal (Compiler)

1. Narita Ahuja
2. Sourav Bebarta
3. Kalyani Abhonkar
4. Kush Gupta
5. Adyashree Ipsita
6. Vanishree
7. Buddha Tamang
8. Varnika Dhawan
9. Deepak Tomar
10. Ujjwal Bansal
11. Radhika Rani
12. Divya Dhanasekaran
13. Kamala Shastry
14. Priyanshi Porwal
15. Neha Chaudhary
16. Paramjit Kaur
17. Shubham Raman
18. Poonam Rathore
19. Navneet Singh Charan
20. Pramesh Kumar

Shubham Shah

(Founder- Flairs and Glairs)

Shubham Shah, an entrepreneur at "Flairs & Glairs" a brand with dynamics in events organizing and cultural educational pan INDIA, is a 26yrs old guy who recently has entered the digital platform of imprinting emotions. He has initiated with his own open mic platform to hel p budding poets and aspiring writers under his brand named as "Teekhe Zasbaaat"

He is a commerce graduate from the Bhagalpur City of Bihar.

He states Writing has impersonated him since childhood and he has now been writing for over a decade!

Cooking, on the other hand, is his passion! He also mentions, trying out new things just tickles him!

When asked sir, Why SPICY EMOTIONS?

He smiled and added, "agar jasbaat teekhe na ho toh wo jasbaat kahan" Spices are all that blends! So do his words!

As a chef, he presents to you his dish! Hot and freshly served! Taste it! Feel it! Enjoy it! You can also find his writing in the Book "Teekhe Zasbaaat" and 50+ Co -authored anthologies. With his passion to explore opportunities across Platforms, he is working with keen dev   otion and We wish him all the very best for his future ventures.

He is Featured in the International Magazine DeMode for his upcoming solo novel.

He is Approved by Ne8x for its Lit Fest, and is a Golden Star Awards 2020 Winner.

He is a India Book of Records Holder for his Anthology Satrang, and has the Grandmaster title by Asia Book of Records, for the same.

He has also been featured in Prabhat Khabar, Dainik Jagran, and a lot of other Newspapers in Bihar for his achievements.

He has been a proud co-author to

India Book Of Records (Title- Black)

World Book Of Records (Title -15 Wonders of Poetries)

India Book Of Records (Title - Aaina)

Vajra World Records Holder (Title - Gustakhi Maaf Hai)

High Range of Records Holder (Title - Gustakhi Maaf Hai)

Indian Book of Records

(Title - Road from Worst to Best)

Share your reviews on his

INSTAGRAM

@spicy_emotions
@shubham4shah

Or via email on

shubham2shah@gmail.com

To stay tuned to his work and opportunities follow his business Handles

INSTAGRAM   FACEBOOK   YOUTUBE

@flairsandglairs
@teekhezasbaaat

WEBSITE:

https://flairsandglairs.in/
https://flairsandglairs.com/

Ishani Agarwal

(Co-Founder- Flairs and Glairs)

Ishani Agarwal hails from the City of Joy, Kolkata.
She is the co -founder of her Community "Teekhe Zasbaaat" and Flairs and Glairs Publication.
Been a Compiler for 45+ Anthologies, she is in the process for more. Co -authored in 150+ Anthologies. She is a India Book of Records Holder, a Vajra World Records Holder, a High Range of Records Holder,   an OMG Book of Records Holder, a Bravo Record holder, a Forever Star Book of World Records and an Indian Book of Records Holder.
Approved by Ne8x for its Lit Fest 2020, and Literary Icon 2020. Also a Golden Star Awards Winner 2020.
She has also been award ed with India Star Republic Award 2021, a part of She Awards by Awards Arc and Winner of Nari Samman 2021 by Literoma.

She is also selected as Best Achiever of the Year by AwardsArc and Most Challenging Compiler Award by Spectrum Awards.
She got her first solo Published,a solo Compilation consisting of first 750 contents of hers, titled "Hand That Burnt While Healing".

She has been featured by the National Magazine "Taree Zameen Par" with the title 'unstoppable'.
Also featured in the International Magazine DeMode for her upcoming solo novel, she is proud to write on social issues, and is happy with the love she is receiving.
Connect with her on Instagram: @Ishani_agarwal_quotes / @compilations_so_far

Sahina Ghugha
(Project Head)

Sahina Ghugha is 20 year old b.com student at Saurashtra university,Rajkot. She is from Jamnagar city of Gujarat. She is Co-author in 50+ anthologies and she compiled 3 Anthologies named "Hoax Feeling's", "Joker" and " Qurbaan". she wants do something for society through her pen.
Insta ID:-
Itz_Sahina_write

Neha Gupta
(Compiler)

As one of the inspired and stimulated JRF aspirant, She has already completed her graduation in B.Com from Satyawati college, University o f Delhi and post graduation in M. Com from IGNOU. She is currently pursuing Bachelor of Education from PMC college, GGSIPU. She has already worked as co-author of 22+ anthologies and Compiler of her own anthologies right now. One of her anthology "Climacterics"selected under Indian Book Of Records. Furthermore, she has started her own Instagram page which is named as itz_neha_writes for motivating depressed and discouraging people.

How An Angel Turns Into Servitude..??

She was an angel,
Born with charming looks;
And splendid mindset....!!
Always dreamt of flying in the sky.
But, lost herself in the midway of callous folks.

She always inclined to be the best dancer.
But, barricaded by savage people;
To maintain solemnity of his family…
She screeched with pain in nights,
And efface her tears till morning…!!

She loves to play football,
But always told that.
Girls are not potent to deal with arduous games;
They are supposed to be play lethargic games only.

She is a proficient, competent,
And most deserving one to be A Doctor,
But no one hold her hand to achieve a big dream...
She begged to support her financially
But, stabbed her ambition in the end.

She was always pretend to do household chores,
For which she become an antagonist.
But still forced to learn it,
As it's responsibility of every girl,
To look for her husband needs first
Even, if she dies from heart to do so.
She supposed to gave up on her ambition,
and bruised her talent for a man,
with whom she has no bonds before marriage.

It was a pleasant day,
When she met to a boy
And, have a crush with him.
It was dazzling, when it instigates.
Like, flying in the sky with open wings.
But, become noxious for her at the end.

When she grew up,
She Loves to hang out with comrades.
But become victim of sexual assault one night…!!
She yelled and become mendicant to insulate herself;
But botched by a gang of molesters.

Her life ends;
But left her footprints in the minds of every girl.
People in crowds knocked at the door of Court for justice.
Lighten the candles everywhere,
But, "Could it get back the life of that little princess…??"
Or "Could it flush out the agony of her parents...??"

Like her,
Many of the twinkle emerged in the cities of India …
Become martyr of heinous crimes from ferocious people.
Still, we called it a democratic country.
And pride ourselves to be the citizens of India,
But, In reality, "Should we....???
Don't know about other views;
But, I never felt pride of being citizen of India,
Where, In modern society of 21st century,
Girls are afflicting brutality of merciless souls…!!

Riya Mandal
(Compiler)

Riya Mandal is a Physiotherapy student, who is a writer at heart. She was born in Kolkata, but raised in various parts of the country. She is currently residing in Cuttack. She loves reading books and listening to music. Being an introvert, she finds solace in expressing her feelings through her words. She wants to make a difference in the world through her creative impressions. All her writings are archived at her Instagram page @inversion_of_words!
Follow her blog
https://lifestylechoicesoverloaded.wordpress.com/

Ever Seen Love?

Love isn't just a four-letter word,
It's a fountain of emotions often unheard!
The sparkle in a mother's eyes
When she hears her child's first cry...
The inexpressible joy of a father
whose little finger is held by his baby daughter...

Love is not just a four-letter word,
It's a fountain of emotions often unheard!
A brother never expresses love for his sister;
But if someone dares to touch her, he turns into a monster...

Love is not just a four-letter word,
It's a fountain of emotions often unheard!
Whenever you are done and dusted with your life;
That solacing touch of your lover gives you the zeal to strive!

Love compels you to feed a poor,
It makes you do everything to please someone dear!
Love is not just a random affair;
It's the saviour in this world of despair!

Love isn't just a four-letter word…
It is everything that helps the world repair!!!

Struggles of a Disabled

I still curse that day!
That day was supposed to be the best day of my life;
After all, I was going to be selected for 'Team India'!
I was so happy and gay...

But my life took a roller coaster fall;
And landed me down in this wheelchair!
I still curse that day!
I was supposed to be a star cricketer,
A hero for my country!
But here I am now, nothing but;
JUST A LIABILITY!

Everyone told me to be brave,
Everyone stood beside me,
Tried hard to hold myself strong!
My mother never spared a drop of tear in front of me!

My father always tried to make me laugh,
But their eyes couldn't hide their anguish;
And that reflection shattered me down!

How I curse my life,
Death would have been much better than this!
Play of destiny is quite bizarre...

I had my whole life ahead;
My Stardust career and,
Tonnes of success!
It all shattered in a moment,
And I faced failure without even an attempt...

No matter how much people say,

about being differently-abled,
The truth is I'm disabled for life!
JUST A LIABILITY FOR ALL!

What 2020 Taught Us?

2020 is considered the worst year of the millennium,
And practically speaking, what's wrong with that?
Some of us lost our loved ones,
Some the good old jobs…
And others quite a lot of memories,
Some potentially precious ones!

But yet I feel 2020 isn't that badass after all;
Because you know what, it taught us the true essence of life,
The value of hope in the times of dismay,
The true faces of people who aren't supposed to stay!
2020 uprooted our lives,
For us to replant a new version of ourselves!
We stumbled, we bewildered, we fell, we stood up…
2020 definitely upgraded us to the next level up!
The struggles we faced throughout the year,
Was definitely worth it!!!

The Game Of Life

What is life?
If not, a game of chess?
Where whether you win or lose,
Depends on the choices you make!

Success and failures are just a part of the race,
But real happiness lies at your mind's pace;
The calmer you are, the better your grace,
What is life? If not, a game of chess?

Making calculated guesses,
Changing plans at every situational mess,
Don't you keep succumbing to the tangled life's direction?
Like the king on a chessboard, surrounded by checks!!!
What is life? If not, a game of chess?

Different characters on the chessboard,
Gives the ideal characteristics to possess,
While crossing across like Bishop is easy,
You need to walk straight like a Rook!

No matter how small a decision is,
Sometimes it can be a game-changing pawn!
Be as royal as the Queen,
Protecting your dear ones, even when you wean and fall!
What is life? If not, a game of chess?

While you stay focused on the win or loss,
What matters is how much you enjoy the challenges at your
call!
What is life? If not, a game of chess?

Impure Struggle of A Girl

I never understood the term purity,
The ironies associated just leave me transfixed,
A girl in her menses is termed impure,
While children are a symbol of purity;
Dalit Women are denied basic drinking water,
And righteousness is claimed as an integral aspect of
pureness;
Love is pure...Isn't it?
But the freedom to choose your lover is impure!
Life is pure, it's divine
But a woman whose husband is dead…
Why the hell should she survive?
I guess this societal notion of Purity
will never get into my mind!
Because every girl is pure, no matter what she decides!

Narita Ahuja

Writing makes her more of herself! Narita is a Japanese word that means to be inventive. Professionally She is a lecturer in Commerce and as an explorer, she has ventured into academics and photography professionally and added to her avocations contemporary dancing, clay modelling, designing and creative writing. As a blogger and a writer, she intends to explore the parallel world of words and take her readers on new adventures in life.

Follow her blog and tell her about her passion for writing at:
https://naritaart.wordpress.com/

Facebook page: NARITART

Instagram: naritaart_

I Am A Plant

Today, while sitting on my yoga mat in my garden and performing Shavasana I gained a thought for my own life. Though I am a nature lover and was so deeply connected to this greenery around, I never realized. The seeds of this plant were sown many years ago by a beautiful couple with a base of vivacious upbringing mud, filling the pot with water every day as several ingredients of life. Sometimes to save this plant from insects and other bacteria, they used pesticides to prevent it from being rotten (ruining), an exemplary life of a child. And was always over -protected through th e shell of care by my parents. So, here I am as a plant in a beautiful vase called home, where my father is a gardener. This is a story of each girl who must have felt the moment of being a serene seed in a colourful pot. I am a plant, inculcating seeds and instil phenomena reaching towards plantations. Plantation of life i.e. planting a life that is mine to rise and shine beyond expectations.

My garden is an evergreen place where 2 more plants grew alongside me i.e. my siblings, blessed with a brother and sister both. Each one of us gets enough sunlight, water, air, in the form of ample care and caution. My gardener made sure that we all grew in the best way possible to cope up with the atrocious world towards nature. He taught us how to stay strong in all the winds like grass on the mud and blossom flowers in times of breeze.

This garden saw all the seasons as I witnessed them every year. These seasons demonstrated the ups and downs, highs and lows in life. Though highs came with happiness and lows made me learn a lot.

Summer is the earliest, the season of existence. Sometimes full of stress and strain as the seed makes the effort to convert into a sapling. Parents take so much pain and worries with just one motive of delivering the best fruits to society. Maybe today the gardener knows the importance of heat for the seed to grow and tomorrow the world will relish the fruits of success in the field of education and the values imparted. Since childhood adding virtues deep in the roots to inculcate the only perfection in life.

Monsoon or rainy season, the season of love, with the abundance of affection and association from the world around me and flowers on me used to share their spirit and smile with the whole garden. The times you want to fly high and touch the sky and your strong will to be out of the shell.

Autumn season, Season of equilibrium, where the plant is taking the shape of a tiny tree balancing each stem and maintaining roots through strengthening virtues of life and imbibing what is right . Building relations and holding them for life by setting a point of equi-balance.

Winter season, the season of care and condition. The process of photosynthesis is continuous but neither visible nor felt to anyone around me where I synthesize food for my soul through modes of self-care by connecting myself to inner peace, not letting the world know what's going inside.

Season of spring where all my leaves get dry and change according to the rules of nature. This is the basis of my spiritualism. With every fall, I achieve a rise with a sense of betterment in my life. Following my faith since childhood that nothing wrong will happen, everything that happens happens for our well being. Now with this thought process, let me give my story a bend. I am 26 yea   rs old, with all my

roots settled in different sections like personal, social, professional, spiritual and even political with a list of norms and regulations to be followed. Being planted in the same garden for more than 2 decades, enjoying every bit of l   ife with a smile and attaining bliss under the shed of other trees, now my gardener has decided to implant me into a new garden. I was in the same vase, same ideology, same thought, same mindset for years, now with the new gardener, and altogether a new pe rsonality and different lifestyle. My mind started questioning if he'll be able to give me the same care, same love, same water and same air to grow.

Like today I'm writing this, it's just the beginning of me as the new sampling in this beautiful garden of flowers. All the plants happily accepted a new member in their chamber and taught this kid that is me the dos and don'ts of our new life. With all the rules and responsibilities, this is the new me in my new home, planning to outgrow and create my small world of bliss again. I have decided to follow the rights and wrongs, complete my duties and share a moment of happiness with everyone. If I am not able to give shade now, I will wait to prosper and initiate no complexity but simplicity to attain eternal peace.
Let the world teach,
 Let the world preach,
People keep their high expectations,
 I live with my simple aspirations.
 I am gonna make a mark on each and everything to my reach.
 I hope, all those of this gender can competently
understand this story of Implant as being one each.

Sourav Bebarta

Sourav Bebarta was born on January 28, 1994. He did his B.Tech in Instrumentation and Control Engineering from ITER college, SOA University. He is currently working as a software developer. He has his own instagram page which goes by the name steelairybreath. He is an avid lover of books and loves reading and writing . His writing style reflects the depth to which he lives and captures life on a day-to-day basis. His favourite pastime remains indulging in writing quotes, Shayaris and short poems as well as musing on life.

Down The Memory Lane

Lately, I have been v ery busy. Covid -19 pandemic has recently begun to spread very rapidly and has compelled me to work from home. Both the house -maid and the cook have been relieved much earlier, leaving me juggling between several tasks at home. Rearing my unruly two -year-old son Runo, looking dutifully after my elderly bed -ridden mother-in-law, doing household chores, cooking meals, and managing all these on the top of my huge pile of leftover office work assignments has slowly started to take a toll on me. I feel claustroph obic and fatigued. More than three weeks of unread mails are lying unnoticed in my Gmail cupboard gathering dust and termites, speaking metaphorically.

Today however I have taken a leave of absence from my hectic pressing work schedule. I could finally spare some time to engage with the bulk of my unread mails. Both Jammie and Runa had been attended to, and they are now fast asleep in their comfy beds under cozy fur quilts. I noticed the hour-hand of the clock had struck 2:00 in the afternoon. I open my MA C languidly, close off a few software update alerts which had popped up unsolicited and finally move on to address the elephant in the room. I log in to my inbox and try to wade through the vast thick sauce of unattended mail which has got deposited unwitt ingly like the memories of my various life experiences tucked away in a secluded corner of my subconscious consciousness.

I quickly realize I have got a very thin time -window for self-indulgence, till Runo wakes up from his utopian fairyland dreams and st arts pestering me, playing mischief. I decided to skim rapidly through the pile – the demon I had fed with my procrastination. The first few items are from the bank

with which I bear a premium salary account, trying to sell me different credit card and Demat account schemes, hoping secretly for me to take a small bite of those forbidden fruits someday by chance. There are a couple of emails from Reedsy – my favorite online author service firm as well imploring me to critique some of the stories from other writers. While scrolling further down, I find quite a handful of mails from Amazon and Flipkart – the two giant e - commerce sites enticing me equally to buy out their latest tech products at the lowest possible market price. Half   -an- hour has gone by. I have   skimmed through most, but also have lent myself to partly scan through a deserving few of the 30 -odd emails I have read uptill now. I keep continuing further headlong ; skimming, and sorting them out with various labels as I deem fit.

In an instant, almos t instinctively, I reverse up the scroll, to get a second look at some familiar term my wandering eyes had barely registered a moment ago among the melee of emails but then lost out to the subconscious will of my marching fingers. I notice a letter that ma kes me stop in my tracks. The subject which was very brief read "Roby – Reconnecting". I open up the mail a bit hesitatingly, my mind starting to run wild in every direction like a forest fire. The email body consisted of only a couple of lines of a single string of indecipherable jumbled -up unusual combinations of characters, numbers, and a few odd emoticons and ancient Roman symbols. I start off on a running verbal monologue of my inner thoughts. Could it be my beloved husband – Robinson, declared MIA by the army during the calamitous Jagal Ghati war with China which took place 2 years ago. Ever since my man went missing, such letters have never ceased coming. Rather, they have increasingly got more believable and improved. I did take them seriously when I had my first tryst with these letters, running from pillar to post, knocking on every open door available of influential people until an investigation initiated suo -moto by the military tribunal finally laid rest to all my expectations and claims after th e mailed letters turned out to be a hoax post examination, leaving me more shattered and broken than before. I remembered how once even a hand-written note had turned out to be a false positive post a thorough examination by a military hand-writing expert.

But I have never before received a letter with cryptic content. I now remember how my beloved husband had taught me the art of cryptography during the early years of my marriage as if he had somehow an inkling about his possible disappearance or even abd uction, seven years before. Memories rush in to flood my mind and I try desperately to connect the dots to get hold of any clue which could give some sense of the happenings, but ultimately, I hit a cul de sac. I then slowly try to recall the methods/rules of decryption which I was closely familiar with in the past and try eagerly to implement it on the task before me. The letter revealed – "DoNT LOsE HOPe. MiSS YOu".

A mixture of emotions pass right through me of sorrow, longingness, anger and finally cul minating in a state of unnatural excitement. But I refrain myself from pinning much hope on yet another letter and taking chances with matters of my heart. Hopes which had got mercilessly crushed in the past had made my heart feeble. After all, someone aga in may be taking me for a ride all along with these cruel sadistic mischiefs. Every army personnel has attended those damn cryptography training camps and even otherwise also, the lessons aren't much onerous to learn for anyone who makes up his mind.

I relapse again into my old fading memories whose comfort I had grown accustomed to, in the haunting absence of my soulmate. Absence makes the heart grow fonder. Not a single day has passed by when I don't remember him with different emotions on different days . I remember the wonderful times we had spent with each other, weaving together beautiful, happy, and loving memories on the soft fabric of my building relationship. I remember how happy he was when Runo was born, almost crying joyously over the call when he first heard the news. I remembered how he got his leave approved soon after and came home to meet little Runo bringing along various fancy toys from all corners of the world. He had decorated Runo's cradle with baby disco lights that he had imported from Japan through a friend of his. I recalled how this joy didn't last very long, as duty soon knocked at the door with loud thumping sounds. I recollect how while the news channels relentlessly played a build -up to the skirmishes and the conflicts we had wi th China, the mighty dragon had already declared a full -fledged war on us, and to get all hands on deck, leaves granted earlier were revoked. Robinson, who has always been as a patriot as anyone else had no choice but to join his mates at the temporary bar racks and bunkers set-up at Jagal Ghati. As a parting gift to me, he had promised to return to me soon, hoping international diplomacy will play a role to help avoid this rampant endless rampage and destruction. But barely five days had passed since he went, that I had received the news of his disappearance from a certain colonel speaking over the phone from the army headquarters situated at Bilto. Soon my fears were found true when the army office officially released the names of all the soldiers who were missing and unaccounted for during this gruesome war at Jagal Ghati. I recollected how, in anticipation of his return, I had refused to mourn and have become gradually stiff by nature as days passed unto months and months into years.

Remembering all these poignant and vivid memories had left me broken, sad, and bitter. As large silent tears started rolling down my cheeks and I tried desperately to hold down those sweet precious memories of which I had very little, suddenly I got alarmed by a loud metallic chime of my cordless doorbell ringing in the distant doorway. Some visitors have come unannounced.

Kalyani Abhonkar

Kalyani Abhonkar a literature student who is still pursuing graduation. She mostly expresses herself with her write -ups. She is from Maharastra, living in the city Nashik. She loves Reading and can spend hours with her books. She hopes one day people will find comfort in her writings just like she finds in the books. Her Instagram page is named @chionophile_1310.

Love Expressed Without Words...

It was two years ago....
I was kinda felt like an outcast, even though it's been three months in this university. Finally, something good happened. When I saw the extra-circular clubs notice pinned on the Bulletin. And I ended up joining a knitting club, even though it's not something that I find interesting. Honestly, I thought, I'll make some friends there and also learn knitting. It sounds horrible, but that's how desperate I was to get rid of my lone - wolf kind of image.
Days later, after finishing all my lectures I went to allotted room. And to my SURPRISE, I saw few guys in. Seeing me, one of them questioned, "Did you join yesterday?"
I gave him a nod. Since,   it's a knitting club I thought, girls probably prefer joining it.
Thankfully, there was a girl too. She was quite a tomboy, yet it was hard to deny that, she was beautiful. She was having long eyelashes and slightly elevated nose Bridge which was hard not, to adore.
"I'm Millie and I joined this club to stop my mom from pestering me for being more feminine. So, knitting will shut her up for sometime."
"Yo, I'm Reyann...Just so you know; I'm the most normal one here. It seems you're kinda surprised seeing guys here. Honestly, you are not the first one."
He continued grumbling...
"Unfortunately, I couldn't help but tag along as I made a mistake. And that's being Neil's friend."
"I was surprised but glad. Why should Art be gender biased? If you like doing something or you are good at something what does gender has to do with it?"
 My statement seemed to impress them.

During all this time someone caught my attention, a guy with greyish-blue eyes.   My stare might have been obvious that Millie noticed it. "He is Neil. He isn't cold as he seems. "

"Neil... I've heard it somewhere... Oh! The scholar who got into fight with the senior few days a go...NOO! Did I say that out loud?" something unintentionally slipped from my mouth. Shit! I shouldn't have said that.

Thankfully, Millie changed the subject. I knew, I was harsh but what made me guiltier was his, not reacting A while later…seeing him in t he parking lot, I called him and apologized.

There were rumors, that he had temper issues. He is rude and difficult to make a conversation with. But surprisingly, we were chatting in the parking lot, almost for an hour.

It was my first meet with them (Millie, Reyann and Neil) but, it never felt like that. From that day, the college life that I've always dreamt of was turned into reality. Having a group of friends, messing up things together and sorting it out together, being friend-zoned by your crush...I never thought, I'll be experiencing all this.

Maybe his looks weird interests, narcissistic nature and over the top intelligence made me fall for him In two years, it might be unbelievable but I've confessed (to Neil) three times...

But, I got rejected.

After, all attempts I made my mind to give up. But, unexpectedly something strange happened. I was chatting on phone with Millie and Neil popped up from somewhere.

"I wanna tell you something." I hanged up the call hearing that "WHAT?" "It's been a while I wanna tell you, I.....I-I........"Now, that was new. My heart was beating crazily and making me nervous as

hell. Yet, I was confused, what made him stuck on ' I '.

"What comes after I..." "I... Common, you know what I mean, don't you?" he scowled" OMG! You're answering my confessions?" "Maybe" he murmured "You're sure you are not rejecting me again?" I questioned unsurely.   "NO..... NOPE" It wasn't expected but his reply was loud and instant. I blushed.

"So does that mean, I should consider you're so called ' I's ' as a yes to my confession?" "Yes" Neil instantly replied. Coming closer he hugged me. It was confusing whether it's he who is confessing or, was it me. I was on cloud nine. I cherish these memories more than anything in life.

Neil may not ex press with words but, confesses his feelings through his actions.   Sometimes words aren't necessary to express your feelings. Many a times, the smallest things we do, makes a person happiest.

Neil saves me a seat if we have a class together...ca   rries my bag, if it's heavy ... leaves me notes (on my locker, and sometimes in my bag)...warns me to eat well...prefers buying cheese popcorn even though he doesn't like them (cause I love them)...These might seem small gestures but, it seems like he is c onfessing his love in every gesture. It's been two years, Neil tried many a times but he is still stuck on his 'I....'.Even if Neil might not use words to express his love, but says it all with his actions.

Love is far more than just expressing your feelin   gs…Even Fathers never express their love. But, will buy an expensive smartphone for his son; while he convinces everyone that he doesn't need such high -tech gadgets for himself   — a basic smartphone will serve his purpose.

When there's love, it naturally ge ts expressed in various unique ways...Enacting expressions of love by learning how to express love is hypocrisy and not love..

Words aren't needed to describe our feelings of Love... :)

Kush Gupta

Kush Gupta is an 18 -year-old theatre actor, a story writer, poet, and a physics, entrepreneurship, and coding enthusiast. He is credited for being one of the host of the International Children's Theatre Festival organized at Talkatora Stadium, New Delhi. H e was one of the 10 students from his school team who won the National Nukkad Naatak competition organized at Bal Bhawan, New Delhi, organized by Ryan Group Of Institutions. He truly believes in exploring and experiencing life in new and fun ways, and foll ows the philosophy given by Elon Musk, "Never give up until either you die or are incapacitated."

Love is Immortal

An extensive scent in the air,
Buzzes trying to declare that ...
you are true, just and wise;
That makes you pure and alive.
A garden breeze is looping your hair;
And you are sitting in a chair
with a smile so wide;
And eyes so clear that
 the sunflowers move towards you dear.
Behind your comfortable smile is ..
a lake as clear as the Nile;
But the sanctity that you beam towards me-
Disembogues into the deepest oceans that
my soul possesses…
I am just a twig on the land floating near
your beautiful hand,
I bow and clearly state to you that
my heart forever beats for you,
The blood that now rushes through my veins makes your
existence flourish in me,
Even though we might have bid adieu-
Yet our souls plunge on to keep
alive our memory…!!

YOU - Your Soulmate

It is a step past the sun, past the vines growing out,
It is a move in the groove, putting the purple & blue far.
It is the stillness of the scenic sky reddish yellow,
It is your beauty both that purifies me, my fellow.
It is the grin that you cast when stumbling blocks are in your way,
It is the ardor that you gather when you are incapacitated.
It is the cry that you master that compels you to transcend beyond expectations
It is the deepest reflection in your eyes that is yielded innately into reality
So let me hold your hand and walk the mile, the mile with stones, the mile with traps,
But a beautiful journey that outlasts the stones because it's the path of life's mile
That I just wish to walk with you and just you,
So remember the journey you seek is seeking you
And beautiful enough that journey is YOU!

The Crux Of A Soldier's Heart

There was once a soldier, who amidst the wartime carved into his outlet diary;
Under a peaceful night, the sky twinkling with beautiful, different- yet indiscriminate- stars.
He wrote a beautiful & enlightening piece for his loved ones expressing what time meant to him,
"A beauty it holds turns out to be a lie.
It is not you but it that passes by!
You say you govern it gracefully,
But it governs the word 'LIFE' itself!
Just as the shapeless water penetrates the atoms of the soil,
It traps your cells in the inevitable, gushing river of its flavors, some sweet, some bitter.
But it has its own exotic vigor.
It is true that a nascent eye will one day reach the beautiful valley,
Where this river will come to a halt,
For all the sunken eyes it carves a glorious shining sun,
That warms the beats of all the hearts that want a seed to treasure.
The seed of memory to its caretakers sprouts a limb of joy and moments of love
Truly Inculcate More Enthusiasm in life
So one can tour all the continually changing addresses of this river with pleasure,
Truly Invest More Energy into life
So your eyes can savor this heavenly flow and serene beauty
Put in a wide frame over your life let this beauty pass through it,
let every new soothing sun cuddle with your mystical eyes,
let the energetic air touch your heart, and cleanse your blood
Portray your honor for it, and
it will make your heart dance along the path of exultation"
The bright and soothing waves of the sun on meeting his skin the next day woke him up,

but also presaged an upcoming conflict between the two equivalents.
He pick ed up his weapons to preserve a piece of his mother earth
which he called his country with pride and fought with all the might
his heart boasted off consequentially getting bruised
taken care of by the army medical staff,
the heavenly moon there in a very godly way
he senses how little time he had, so while getting healed he again expresses his heart out to loved ones "Approaching end is a way to search for truly blooming flowers which shall beautify the garden's meaning,
Care for it to be more green and nourishing, to be at its best,
To find means to convert each soothing drop of dew, each bruising sand storm, each ray of sun to each ray of hope, each storm to teach the garden to find its integrity, each soothing drop to let it grow more each day.

Life is beautifully unpredictable, it's true, but life is also unjustifiably lovely to live."
The next dawn, the war took to its extremities and his fellow soldiers started facing defeat and retreated. It was such a horrible situation that even the temporary   army healing camps were under attack - as was his. Yet, he fought the enemy to the mightiest pinnacles of his strength. Killed everyone - but due to his injuries being quite harsh he fell to the ground, only to witness glimpses of his 3-year-old daughter and wife, to breathe out his last words facing the mirage of his daughter:
"It would be a shame to vanish without letting this Earth witness what our heights of physical and mental perseverance have in store to serve it dutifully."
There was once a soldier, who changed the lives of all his readers.

Adyashree Ipsita

Adyashree Ipsita is a budding writer hailing from Odisha
pursuing her under graduation from a well -known university.
She loves to unite the pen and the paper with her thoughts
and create something really unique. She has always been
fascinated with literature and is an ard ent learner. As a teen
she is associated with an NGO and serves a strong support to
the youth of the era. Despite being busy with her studies and
various work schedules, her passion for writing never faded.
Her way of perceiving life makes her really special.

The Solitude Distorted

Autarky is a grace,
No matter any soul you face.
Alone we rise,
Longing for an angel in disguise.
Alone we doze,
Almighty's plans are ready- he's just waiting to impose.
Alone we come down,
Relishing profiles with frown.
Alone we get into vehicles of thoughts,
Swotting regarding aughts.
Assistance approaches for hoisting us,
A support system anchored alike truss.
Lending a helping hand to one another,
In the daily life toiling together.
Jointly sobbing,
Hankering about the memorable chuckling.
Together we crawled so we brawled,
Union yawned adding a thousand-fold.
Brothers pave the pavements,
Accomplishing all achievements.
Sisters love from heart,
Arguments cannot draw her apart.
Affection stitched adoration,
Incarnating siblings' dedication.
Family is a farrago,
Forbearance stows in doggo.
Calmness and kindness gently sown,
Each one untouched on their own.
Strings of warmth assemble a duvet,
Merriment fabricating an asset.
Bonds valued more than jewels,
Tender and adores accruals.
Cherish the recollection of years,

Audaciously vocalize- here's the brood of ours.
Tales told for the little nods,
Stand together and overcome all odds.
Clench craving, told sightly,
Gazing at the delicious dishes gummily.
Hold hope for all,
Parts of life-these rise and fall.
Harvest happiness for each,
Longing for all's well being, we preach.
Invest inspirations-a life's lesson,
These are the veracities not the treason.
The thy is all-over,
Everyone thus adore.
He manifests the alley,
Organized with orders and survey.
Notifies all,
Awaking with an advise call.
Illuminates the illusion,
Executes every reason.
A teaching meant to be,
But a command from thee.
Do not stand at our grave and weep,
We are not there, we are not asleep.
We are the wavy winds that flow,
We are the diamond glints on snow.
We are the sunlight on the ripened grain,
We are the gentle and sober autumn rain.
Do not stand at our grave and cry,
We are not there, we did not die.
Together we are and always will be,
That's an instruction from the almighty.

Life Metanoia

It is a mountain,
Its steps are a fountain.
Our dreams are its interpretations,
Accomplishing ambitions announces narrations.
It isn't easy, you know,
It's all hailstorms here before the snow.
Circumstances changing conversely,
Clinching calms consequently.
It is a tome,
Its episodes are a loam.
Stumbling blocks make an interference,
The almighty holding up as an adherence.
It isn't ideal, you know,
It's all test here before the result they show.
Hailing habitat hazily,
Handling hope happily.
It is queer, with ups and downs,
Illuminating concerning all grounds.
Twists and turns round the way,
Nature's serenity they display.
It isn't unadorned you know,
It's all illusion before the artwork lying below.
Pain's paving passively,
Preaching positivity possessively.
It is a burnished brew of…
Your confidence and credence,
Your perspectives and reliance.
It is an accessible account of…
How honest you are,
Who is your shimmering star.
It has no definition, it's ne'er the same,
Poles apart it's unique for every frame.
Notes and tones express it over fife,
Jingling every essence cleped as life

A Hiraeth Found

It all started with monsoon rain,
Braiding down the window pane.
Thunders rattled and met the downpour,
Two golden hearts clashed to make a soul conquer.
Duo orbs linked up,
Mutually glancing at each's blub.
Convening endurance to express emotions,
Both pondering about each other's reactions.
The night-time concluded on glace gesture,
Holding up this affectionate vesture.
Wandering all night regarding the pair's beauty,
Dreaming of the upcoming duty.
The following morn initiated,
Sun was tamed but the cloudy noon baited.
The duo waiting for coincidence once again,
Gradually the almighty commenced the rain.
Showers made them united,
The torments were confiscated.
The jeweled drops patted the pairs calmly,
And the hearts hoped humbly.
Twains embraced, confessed and gifted flowers,
Rightly said love is in the air when it showers.
Because…
Braiding down the window pane,
It all started with monsoon rain.

Vanishree

She is an introvert,
But her instinct makes her an extrovert,
The small voice inside her insists her to a convert,

Finally, changes her anxious heart into a calm and peaceful art".

A teen named Vanishree, wandering for opportunities with simple quotes. She is a pessimist. She will always be going for immortal things.

Struggles And Scars

"Experience all kinds of pain,
Nothing will be going vain,
All thoughts will be running in
the head like a wine,
Try to survive without getting ruin,
Let it be too much of rain,
Let everything look uncertain,
Become a dangerous one to refrain from everything and be
yourself ".

The scar in the heart for love in the rain will never go vain.
Sometimes it will be bleeding more with blood for the whole
life and time heals, where it becomes the routine.

No one will be there, nothing will give you hands except the
pain of love. The nostalgic memories of togetherness will
tear you apart to lubricate your scar.

At times the pain of scars will be expressed through
weightless tears, and you will start to experience your world
of darkness of love

The scar will become bigger and deeper with exquisite pain
and will make you ready for anything. Who knows, you may
even be grateful to your scar at the end for the change in you!!

This is going to be the fate of life for everyone, and it's up -to
you to make the king's move to be queen of your life with
scars!! Wait for your time and be grateful for your scars.

Struggles and pains are the real things triggering our talents
to test our patience.

Patience, in the sense, emptiness of mind. Difficult but needed.

Always the things we need will be there in front of us, we just need to wait for it to make our mind not blind to it further.
We just need to have a little wit to find and understand it...
Just do what you can... enough.

Love

'Be benevolent by heart and miser in hate'.
Fall in Love to experience life. Love is an immortal book where there is no end for it, where the pages will be going for an eternity.

Joining of two souls is what love is, not bodies. It is a weapon for two disciplined souls to adhere to principles. Where you will feel yourself as a newborn with loyalty and selflessness.

Nostalgic memorie s of togetherness will heal your heart at times when tears seek its path towards you.

Love is a feeling, which can be extremely true and honest, which will make you ready for anything, and it's rare.

It will hurt at times and make you feel alive all the time. You can feel your soul, always whispering its purpose for its loved one in your ears.

Everything is real and has no boundaries here, a genuine and gut path is what love is, just for your loved one with your blood and soul.
You will make secret promises to yourself about love.

Your achievements will be beyond anything, as a divine soul chosen by God to lead a pure life like swans with one partner for love.

Your life will become a pearl in a deep shell of a sea. It's a feeling to imagine giving your life for him truly without expectations, even in his absence.
life is not immortal but love is....
A bed of fragmented glasses is what love is, only persons with pure heart and true love can sleep in it as like a solace.
Make true memories of love, li ve your life spending with it and do your part truly from heart!

Failure And Secrets

We are given freedom to think whatever we want, but only when we think according to our principles we can be at peace. A person who manipulates that freedom of thinking wins life.

Extremely complicated and excruciating thoughts are the biggest enemies. The most difficult thing in life is the silence of the mind, there are traps in thoughts.

You must be clever enough to not fall into traps.
There is a fool and a contra st in you, don't make them fight with each other.
Give yourself enough time to recover from abnormal to normalcy through silence of mind.

It's based on the principles you adhere to and the practices for spiritualism. You need to wait for your time,, hopef ully. Waiting or trying again is going to be the right path.

"Long time buried soul's secret, a thousand secrets of pain and happiness behind the smiling face and aching heart. Can it be revealed?

Making us sleepless and a Philosopher of life. Uncovered laughs and hidden cries with a heavy heart of darkness are our secrets?

Where these secrets are revealed through writings to flourish the life of others. Where combination of his/her pains and happiness becomes their identity.

Fragmentation of a person's heart is always the highest secret which can be expressed through tears and writings!!

Keep having more secrets and lubricate those through writings"!!

Success

There is a fruit which will be ripened only when a person is squeezed, devastated, abandoned and humiliated even after then he has to be consistent in his tasks and patience plays a vital role there, after all of it he can taste that ripened fruit which is called success. Just to satisfy his born obligation.

Fragmentation of a person's heart will bring itself to success. You need to pay for your hard work with patience and a broken heart with passion for success!!

Where tears will break you apart, where your thoughts will make a cunning play to crook your path, but the winds of success dreams soothe your soul!!

Buddha Tamang

Buddha Tamang was born and brought up in Delhi, India. He is currently working as a security concierge in Doha, Qatar. He is inspired to become a prominent writer. So, he writes poems, quotes, and short stories. He shared the "struggles of a dreamt child"during his childhood in the anthology named 'Beyond my expectation'

Struggles Of A Dreamt Boy

A 12 -Year-old boy named, Buddha Tamang inhabiting the mountainous part of Nepal, who was inspired by his brother to become an 'Indian Soldier'. But, due to poor education in his town, his brother decided to took the boy to India. And, he stays within four walls of the "Ex -commander's house" where only Ex -commander and his wife lived together. The boy's brother had made an agreement with the "Ex-commander" that he'll stay with them and his needs are fulfilled by them until he grew up. And, then He will be recruited by them as a soldier. The boy had no idea about that he had to stay with them as a "maid", and he could not go to School to accomplish his Goals of life. All he was supposed to do is household chores in the day   -time and study during the morning only from 5'o clock to 7'o clock.

After completion of one year, the boy slowly realized that he lost his childhood and become slave of Ex -Commander and his wife. He wants to run away but couldn't as he was neither educated nor financially independent. He alw ays went to bed exhausted at the end of the day just to jump up the next morning to sit on the same study table to get hands on the books. When he woke up in the morning, he wants to have pleasure of listening sounds of birds chirping, and noises of little children who are playing in the ground. But, he couldn't as he has to look for the demands of Ex Commander and his wife. Apart from this, He had to manage his studies as well within a short span of time.

Two years passed, And he started thinking that, "Is   this the way to live…?" Or "Is this the life….??" where I haven't had any option except to sacrifice my childhood and studies to fulfill needs of my future. He could go on holidays only with those brutal souls, but have no life with his peer group as a little boy. He couldn't play, eat, study and have fun with those little kids. Furthermore, he always missed the love of

his caring mother and father, as no person can replace theirs love. No one can felt the same way as he did in the arms of his mother. When ever he looks outside from window of car, that other children are cuddling with their parents. He also felt desire of it.

When he entered into the age of teenage, He started becoming conscious of himself. He cared for the freedom of himself and refused to put restrictions on him by others. One day, He took scooter of Ex Commander and move outside to feel the fresh air, birds chirping, noises of vehicles, delicious food. He has enjoyed his freedom for the first time, as he is alone during that day. He felt down, but rouse up again because he knows that "no can grew up without falling down" in his life.

On the next day, when Ex Commander woke up and look at the scooter. He found that all the parts of a scooter are broken into pieces. And Ex Commander scold the   little boy badly. The boy tried to save himself but couldn't as no one else is there to do such acts. At that day, he decided to move out of this hell and gave a thumbs up to his career. He had taken back to his home by his brother and get admission into   the prestigious school. He admitted to "level -08" in the school after qualifying some tests by toiling himself for day and nights. But, he still felt unsuccessful as he missed his childhood and many more great opportunities in his life.

Varnika Dhawan

Varnika Dhawan is a 12th -Grade student who's a bibliolater, and an enthusiast novice writer. Curating critical feelings, sentiments, and atrocities of adolescents and through words giving rise to an explanation is what counts on her skil   ls. Messy, ambiguous, ethically fraught questions that are part of teenagers' lives
heartens her to write. Notice how the part of the story is used to support this discussion.
Instagram ID- varnika_dvn
varnikadhawan4@gmail.com

Chemical Bodies, Dopamine Hearts

He was a beautiful flesh of millions of piled-up atoms.
After fourteen, the body explores bountiful dopamines and
hormones.
 He let his eyes run over me a little and then looked away. He
turned reddish from my intermittent staring.   I stayed around
him for four days, but I still don't remember if it was the
family gathering or any event for which I was there. His
curled smiled with a nasty look would turn me on.
One fine day –wait, not a fine day, a desirous, a yearning day,
we were watching T.V., exhausted. I was a psycho, then   —
Wondering and wandering—Tripping on daydreams with
untied laces. I asked him to play any channel of porn. He did.
We watched it very casually and then went in our own
directions. It was typical for him but we ird and nice for me.
He knew I was somewhat nymphomaniac. I developed a
strong infatuation with Him.
I became a maladaptive daydreamer, imagining him in my
wildest fantasies.

I was asleep on a couch in the living room with brassiere
dangling out of the planks and my legs wide opened. He
walked into the kitchen to make coffee. It woke me up. After
looking at me like that, how he is still not into me, I thought.
He jerked his neck in the most uninteresting way to check out
when I accidentally brushed my leg against his. I greeted him
with the ridiculous pickup line I could ever say. "Have I died
and gone to coffee heaven?" I said, rolling my eyes in an
alluring look, just like Ana stasia gives to Christain Grey in
Fifty Shades of Grey. "Because you seem like a coffee angel,
Kinosb" I moaned.

  "Kaira, it'd be a 'Brain heaven.' That's your requirement.
Be mature," he grimaced.

His pickup line was better. It shattered me. He clench   ed his teeth. I now loathed his accurate jawline which I loved the most.

 It's not a cliché kind of broken love story. It happens whenever I am around my crushes. Crushes literally screw your brain, your spirit, your confidence but not your body that you want to be screwed.

"Edge of Seventeen,
Literally devastating.
Broke, Nasty, Stoned, Tripped
With active pleasurable wrist.
Stalkers of Love, a vocabulary of grunts
Sulky, fucking perverts.
 Wild, Nutty, Wacky
Mind roaring, shrieking, diving,
The teenage angst Desperately
In hunt of limbo meanings."

Teenage is a phase of humans characterized by spatial unawareness and a copious amount of masturbation. Their world is always bleak. Their life goes in limbo. You wander for finding meaning. And from ages, you could have found that meaning, but your bodies' chemical trap has always hindered you to do so. That chemical trap is what makes a teenager 'A teenager'.

In my early sixteen, I'd discovered something much Bizarre; First Kiss and Self Love. By the way, it was also the age when I finally decided to get a sight of nakedness. That kiss misled me by the fact that he was the comprehendible love I was hunting for.
 I felt him as a prince to my Cinderella or my Snow -white or fucking meaning to my useless life. It ended up with a modest realization, prized from my maturity box that opens

rarely, that Alice was never in the wonderland; that neither the crystal glass s hoe was ever fitted to Cindrella nor that prince's kiss made Snow white alive.

It's just a cute fairy tale that has reality contradictions. No one tells that dumb -wit part where Cinderella wanted the BJ and Prince couldn't satisfy her. So she wished from that same lady godmother, who had turned the pumpkin into a coach from the wave of her wand, to turn the Cucumber into You - Know-Who.
My infatuation became unaccountable and uncontrollable. My chemical body was fizzing with these bubbles of abnormalities.

We were high on booze. Being Seventeen entitles one for boozing, I thought. That night I started believing in wonders. While making *Chai* for neutralizing our intoxications, we were bounded on that emotional attraction of fondness towards each other's sa rcasm and behavior. He finds me cute and cool when I'm drunk . What if I become Kabir Singh when He'll leave me? Would he still find me cute? Because I didn't find Kabir Singh, the modern version of 'Devdaas', at all cute. He became stupid when Preeti left him, I thought, staring straight into His eyes but tonight, not with that pretentious Anastasia's look but with my own adoring kiddish peeks.

To my astonishment, He expanded His arms on both sides and grasped me from my shoulders. That was the cutest hug but weird because I wanted him to hold my waist. We hugged for 22 seconds How could I forget that seconds? Hug from my love!! I too clasped my hand over him passionately and embraced him softly but a bit tight, unable to comprehend what's just happening. I should release him now, maybe I am becoming inappropriate , I thought. The moment

I loosened my grip, He traced his lips over my forehead. They were softer than cushions.

Chemical was reacted with a strong salt now. There was no way the reaction could be reversed. It exploded with effervescent bubbles rushing, dashing, fizzing, and humming—oh god—I'm dead— should I kiss him now— he's scary, he's 20—What if I felt inappropriate? –or what if I became inappropriate? I was shivering. I got wet. Till the time I could decide anything he unclutched me.

At 5 a.m. I asked him to follow me outside the house to get the sight of sunrise. He got me. Sunrise's obviously a hint.

He whispered, "there's too much risk, Kaira. If we get caught by someone."

The reaction was extinguished. It was failed. I was again shattered.

"Kinosb, What are you saying? Why would our family mind if we watch the sunrise? Are you out of your mind? Fine. I'll go by my own," I slurred my words.

We assign passionate importance to things when we are young because we don't have that breadth of experience to behave moderately. Thus, we sully love with desperate attractions and carnal desires. And failing to understand this, we sit around and pine and become miserable for the rest of our Juvenile-fucking-life. We don't use social empathy to make friends instead create a depressing element — Loneliness that's always ready at the doorstep of our darkness to fuck our lives. And loneliness sucks you harder than BJ.

We literally manufacture an existenti al crisis out of thin air. At the dawn of teen, we're pulled in many directions while discerning whether those brand new feelings are more like "flashes of lightning" or an "eternal ocean".

Teenage life situation has been beautifully explained by Rashid Ali –
"Kabhi kabhi toh lage zindagi mein rahi na khushi or na maza,
 Kabhi kabhi toh lage har din mushkil Aur hare ek pal ek saza
Aise main koi kese muskuraye or kaise hasde khush ho ke,
 Or kaise koi soch de, Everything's gonna be ok."

 It's all a blam e of age scale, we're not faulty. It shall pass. We can be the kings of Adrenaline. Incur that all desperations and fight it.
Now, I've lost my all interest in Him. I wish I could've gone to my past Kaira, explaining to her that, "you'll get a lot of chances to allure 'Many' with Anastasia's looks and better pickup lines. You don't need to stick on one. Just go with a flow."

Let's conflate optimism with servitude; "If Vasco da Gama could travel 2400 miles to discover the route to India, out of Seven billion Humans out there can't I find one route to Someone's heart?"

Deepak Tomar

Deepak tomar was born and brought up in Delhi, India. He completed his graduation and post graduation from one of the renowned university, University of Delhi. He has experience of 10 yrs of working with Multi National Company as an Accountant. He always fervour to write poetry and short story to express his thoughts.

Unpleasant Taste Of Life ...!!

It was the story of a poor boy, who bor   n and brought up in the capital city 'Delhi' of India, one of the illustrious place also known as "The heart of India".

He was always an aspiring and dedicated child for his studies. Due to poor family background, he can't afford to have education from renowned and well established school. He just took admission in Government School due to lack of financial support. And, prefer to do part -time job along with his studies to earn some pocket money to fulfill his basic needs...

He always dreamt to be best cricket player of India, but never achieved so due to lack of support from his family. He always loves to bunk classes for practice of cricket to accomplish his dream, but his heart was broken when he sacrificed his dreamt to be bread earner of his family.

He worked in KFC to earn some pocket money in early stages. But, later decided to be employee of MNC company as a Chartered Accountant which is considered as one of the eminent profession in India. Apart from this, he always dreamt to have a billion doll ars in his pocket. He burnt himself in darkness of night to proselytize his vision.
But could not be able to achieve it, as he is a poor boy and always looked out to serve the needs of his family first.

One day, He met to a girl who offered him books of accounts freely and asked him to keep it with you. He, always as an ambitious person, decipher language of those books and capture each and every concept in his eyes.

And, that proves to be the turning point of his life…

After that, he applied for a ju nior accountant post and got a selection in one of the prestigious MNC company. He finds himself in the light of sun after receipt of an offer letter from that Company. He can't express his happiness at that moment. He just become a speechless person for few hours.

But, that's not enough for him to be a successful person of his life. He wants to prove his talent in front of the whole world. He also joined a coaching for UPSC preparation, but failed to clear it at last stage.

Instead of his busy schedule , he always managed to finished syllabus within a short span of time…

Meanwhile, he also get to indulge in share marketing, which is one of the way for him to become a billionaire. At the end, he finds share marketing so interested that he never looked back for any government job. He starts investing in share marketing and become a champion of that.

He read some of the books of share marketing leader, i.e. Warren Buffet… And, learnt the best techniques to handle share marketing.

Today, he is one of the best player of share marketing.

He proves that …
"If you are determined to accomplish your goals, no one can stop you."

He met to the same girl, who off ered him books few years back, which was just a co incidence… And thanked to her for always being a warm-hearted girl...!!

Ujjwal Bansal

Ujjwal Bansal was born and brought up in Uttar Pradesh. He loves music and meeting new people. He loves writing articles to motivate youth and inspire them to fulfill their dreams. All his articles are posted on his Instagram handle @escortyouthdreams

Can Friendship Turn Into A Relationship?

Friendship is a bond of trust. In this bond, we can share anything without any embarrassment. We don't even have to think for a second before sharing anything with our friends! Friends always support us and when we are wrong, they tell us that we are wrong. Friends are of two types: fake friends and true friends.

A fake friend always supports you even in your bad deeds. They stay with you in your good times but not in your bad times. On the other hand, true friends always support you when you are right but they do not support you when you are wrong. True friends may not stay with you in your good times but they will be with you in your bad times. You may forget those friends who stay with you in your good times but never forget those friends who stay with you in your bad times.

The Friendship Between A Boy And A Girl Is The Best!

The friendship between a boy and a girl is the most beautiful relation according to me because they share a different bond. A boy can share those moments and stuff which he cannot share with his male friends while the girls can   also share all the moments with his male friend which she cannot share with her female friends. In our society, people might think that they are not friends but couples who are going to be committed soon! And they will get married afterward! Because of this, many problems occur between them. Due to societal pressure, their parents start thinking that both of them are in a relationship. They stop them from meeting each other, convince them that both of them are not good for each other. Soon, because of all the societal comments, one of the people in the friendship starts thinking that he loves the other and differences start occurring in their bond.

Me AND MY BESTIE

My bestie is my Mr. Bean. She understands me very well! She is an idiot but she is my   idiot! She looks cute when she gets angry. I have named her Colgate advertiser as she keeps advertising her teeth all the time. She is reserved for me so anyone who tries to take her away from me, will face dire consequences! I will break every single bon e of that person. She is very special to me and that's why I want to cherish our friendship forever! We don't want that if we come into a relationship, our friendship breaks or suffers.

I will give some advice to you guys, if you have feelings for your b estie, make sure that if you guys come into a relationship, your friendship does not break. I feel that friendship is the most beautiful relationship in the world because in friendship we can share anything with our friend without any fear of being judged. Our friends never judge us but our partners may judge us sometimes.

Message For The World!

If you fall in love with your best friend don't expect anything from him or her. Don't assume that they will say only yes to you as they are your best friend. Friendship and love are different and both the relations have their own importance. Even if you get into a relationship with your best friend, make sure that you don't forget you were friends first! Don't let things change between you and your bestie. I know the shift from friends to couples is not easy. So it is not compulsory to behave as couples yo u can keep behaving like friends. The only difference is that both the friends get some rights to each other like kissing and cuddling. Don't feel insecure if your friend is talking to others like some people do when they are in a relationship. You are bes t friends first and then couples. You know your best friend's nature and everything about him or her, so don't feel insecure at all! Little jealousy is okay because that is the sign of love. Over jealousy is otherwise named insecurity. Be jealous but don't be insecure!

Take advantage that you are friends before being couples. Don't take it as a disadvantage that you are friends first and then couples. By saying, we are a couple now and not friends, don't make the circumstances different. If you guys don't make it differ ent, I promise your relationship will become stronger and no one will be able to break it. Because now you are in a double relationship, first as friends and then as a couple.

Radhika Rani

An Artist, Radhika Rani, is born and brought up in Kerala. She did her graduation in civil Engineering. Since her college days, She developed her skills in painting and drawing. She also developed her skills in different activities as painting, folk art, photography, poetry and motivating and self questioning couplets.

Flameless Smoke

Captured in divinity the child came
Small steps first, she took for the path ahead
Strides took carefully to the way she aim

Rested her belief as her name got inked
Rejoicing in pamper of her wedlock
As the lumber floating along it irked

Washing dusting cooking around the clock
Ceased to check the blemishes on her mass
Dusting bedding shredding in her old clothe

Emotive idle moments of her crass
Let her fire burn from inside all smokeless
Flameless smoke came out of her enraged wrath

Laid to rest her peace to fight for herself
Paid for the breath of fresh air she walked free.

Raining In Summer

Change of seasons or wrath of Mother Earth?
Cloudy sky in the midst of hot summer
Charged with thunder and lightning in the night

Deep oceans churned from above and beneath
Days of the dead that about to arrive
Dreams shaken a bit but never it broke

Bloomed in the midst shower the deep desire
Buried in the seeds of courage to heal
Bounced the will of imagination it derive

Rains in this summer drenched the seed to peel
Rested under the soil it spread the wings
Remnants unite to give life in this isle

Sprang from nowhere with the airborne scent fresh
This unknown weed, to paint the ground yellow.

Faith, Hope ,Dreams

Locked us inside the tessellate in concrete
Loved once afar out of reach for a touch
Left with self in the shelf of our innate

Countless steps that go up nowhere to reach
Counting hour's minutes seconds as it pass
Cloudy as it got in this midsummer March

Drained the hope of faith left moments toss
Disposed the immediate in this cuboid
Days of respite yet the garden blush in rose

Wounds that might heal leaving the keloid
Weighing the heaviness of our dreams
Withstanding all odds in this time of discoid

Faith, hope and our dreams to lean over
Fair is the war to thrive, sustain in our innate.

"मैं, तुम और वक़्त हमारा"

एक अरसा हुआ रहती है कुछ कमी सी है अब हर पल में मेरे,
यादों के झरोखों से झाँकते हैं वो लम्हे साथ के तेरे,
लहरे भी मायूस हो लौट जाती हैं किनारे से,
गूँजती नही हैं यहाँ हँसी अब जो तेरी ।
रेत भी हो चली है रेख़्ता,
तरस गयी पाने को आहट क़दमों के तेरी ।
ढलती शामें भी अब खामोश सी हैं,
इंतज़ार में सुन ने को फिर से कोई कहानी तेरी ।
सागर का वो किनारा भी पूछता है अब तो,
"कहाँ बिछड़ गये वो यार जो कभी चलते थे हाथ थाम कर ??"
 खाली राहें भी थक गयी हैं अब तो तेरा रास्ता निहार कर ।
चल अब मैं तोड़ू समय की गुल्लक, इक्कट्ठे कर कुछ सिक्के तू भी
फुर्सत के ।
पूरे कर आयें वो किस्से अधूरे, ज़माना हुआ नहीं मिले हम खुल के,
चल सजाएँ फिर एक रंगीन शाम, इस भागती दुनिया से छुप के,
खोलें यादों की अलमारी, छेड़े फिर कोई बात पुरानी,
सागर किनारे सिंदूरी सांझ में, फिर से हम यूं हाथ थाम कर
देखें फिर वो सूरज ढलता, मैं, तुम और वक़्त हमारा ।

"यूँ ही"

कभी यूँ ही कुछ कहे बिना चुप रहना अच्छा लगता है ।
सिन्दूरी होती साँझ में सागर किनारे,
देखना लहरों पर वो सूरज पिघलते,
सुनना सुकून से तेरी ख़ामोशी
बिन बोले तेरी धड़कन से बातें,
तेरे एहसास में बह जाना अच्छा लगता है ।
कभी यूँ ही कुछ कहे बिना चुप रहना अच्छा लगता है ।
रख कर तेरे कांधे पर सर,
ठहर जाती हैं बातें इन अधरों पर,
छोड़ सवाल अन्तर्मन के,
बैचेनी जग की सब बिसरा कर,
तेरी बाहों में खो जाना अच्छा लगता है ।
कभी यूँ ही कुछ कहे बिना चुप रहना अच्छा लगता है ।
गहराती रात के आलम में,
साथ लिए तेरी यादों के साये,
अपनी तन्हाई से वो तेरी बातें,
तेरी यादों मे खो कर यूँ ही,
इस दर्द को सहना अच्छा लगता है ।
कभी यूँ ही कुछ कहे बिना चुप रहना अच्छा लगता है ।

Dhivya Dhanasekaran

A budding writer with a million unanswered questions in her eyes. She began writing because she realized that the world needs to see the light from the words. Currently, pursuing medicine, her hobbies are writing, reading, and dancing. She practices dance in all forms with great grace and a tint of magic. She is one of those brave people who reflects the reality in her writing.

I See You Through Your Days.

I have seen you smile,
laugh out loud, go goofy around,
hold your tummy in pain when you laugh,
your cheeks turn cherry red when you laugh,
your eyes hold all the happiness the world has seen and
you pass that on to every person walking by.

You send your love and happiness like the breeze,
that falls on everybody's face without any hesitation.
I have seen you look at romance and smile,
dream of love when you sleep.
I have caught you smiling at random moments,
and I know it is because he was running on your mind,
or perhaps you kissed him at that second in your head.

I have seen you water that plant, because you saw its
sadness.
You smiled at it and you saw it smile back.
You watch the colours of the sky and they make it look even
more beautiful
because you love watching them and the skies saw your heart
smile.
I have seen you sing lyrics and relate to your love.
I have seen you selfless,
staying awake and hoping to be the last face he will see.

You want to be his smile;
you want to be his everything.
I have also seen you cry because you had to put yourself to
sleep.
I have seen you sit still in the stairs of that huge building,
and watch everything around with sadness in your eyes.

Your eyes would show sadness and the skies wouldn't change
colours that day,
but instead show your favourite shade.

The sky would gleam itself in lilac streaks,
and it would calm your soul.
That man in the cafe,
would add a little more sugar in your coffee,
and it would soothe your pain.

Your best friend would stay silent, she would understand,
she would say, it was okay,
you were still the best girl she has ever known,
and that guy should actually feel bad for letting you be sad.
you would see how this girl loved you,
and how much she made sure you were okay.

Every part of your world would lend you extra smiles
to put that happiness in your eyes,
because the world knew what beauty me ant- the happy eyes
of yours.
But you are still worried
About that one guy that thinks you are the mistake.

He just seems to forget how much you love him,
and all he thinks is that you have no home,
and will eventually fall to him.
This is to the girl, I have been seeing every day,
you are different in every eye that see you,
but to me you are the most perfect, beautiful,
and the kind of girl every person craves for to hold by their
side.

Your beauty is in your eyes that carry happiness,
your aura that is so much peace, joy and comfort.

That guy may or may not know
how to love you right or how much valuable you are.
But there is that evening sky, the moon,
 the stars, the birds, the colours, the Bougainville flowers
that fall to your feet, that extra spoon of sugar that believes
it makes you happy, the waters in the pond
that await your arrival every day, that want your happy eyes.

They all know your love
They all know your happiness
They know your vibe
They know your aura
They know how much you light up this world.
I envy you for being everyone's favourite.
But I wish you are your favourite too.

 -with love, the gi rl that is trying to fall in love with herself
and trying to emphasize this fact by writing it to herself.

Kamala Shashtry

Kamala is a retired school teacher with 34 years of teaching experience in Fatima High School at Ambarnath, near Mumbai. She is also an Art of Living faculty, teaching the Happiness Program. An avid reader and a poet at heart. She is a great friend, a r ole model of her students. A kind and sensitive person. The Art of Living now epitomizes her sole purpose of living. Her hobbies include drawing, painting and music. Her poems are an interpretation of pleasant revelation of the simple facts of life, ex periences and through her Guru's teachings.

Love

Love is not an emotion,
It's personified.
Earth's gravity embraces you;
The sun kisses you warmly,
Nature's unconditional love,
Rains shower the earth's bosom.
Love has myriad colors and flavors.
I love you just because …
You are, you, and I am I.
Love sighs, seduces, cajoles,
Stirring your passions, embracing,
Your loved ones, close to your bosom.
There is no two, you are united forever,
In mind, body and soul.

The Yearning

Oh love, take me yonder,
where the sky meets the earth.
A romantic drive on a lonely road,
just you and me.
The wind blowing in our faces.
The sun kissed us his warmth.
The trees passing by.
Take me to the pristine beach,
running barefoot on the cool sands,
the waves kissing our feet.
Watching the waves dancing.
The gulls flying above, a symphony in the sky.
The setting sun, casting a golden glow,
a beautiful masterpiece, in the heavens above.
Come, lets soar high with ecstasy.
 Just You and me.

Beyond Expectations

I met you, and my life changed forever.
I never thought, I would meet someone.
It's my Beloved ONE, my world.
When the universe brought us Together,
There's some meaning to it.
Otherwise, why would we meet?
We were strangers in this journey of Life.
Brought together by providence,
We will walk this path, and heal each other.
I am grateful to have you in my life.
You brought meaning to my life.
It's so comforting to be with you.
You complete me completely,
Two Imperfect Souls Come Together
Soul to soul connection.
Twin flame journey in this life.

Stepping Stones.

They say failures are stepping stones to success.
Avoid being discouraged if you fail.
Once, twice,many times.
Remember, Thomas Edison,
So many trials and tribulations.
Or so many inventors.
It's only when he was tired,
He sat under an apple tree.
He apple fell on his head.
Isaac Newton discovered gravity.
The rest is history.
Even Archimedes, relaxing in a bathtub,
And he had an Eureka moment, isn't it?
Never be bogged down by failures.
People may throw stones or brickbats,
Use them to your advantage.

Life Is Magical.

Life is magical and mystical,
We live only Once,
Make it worthwhile.
Avoid regrets or glorification.
Avoid negativity and anxiety, about your future.
Acceptance of people and situations as they are.
Save your mind at any cost.
Life is a miracle,a blessing.
We should be grateful every moment.
Keep smiling come what may.
Life has no rewinds and forwards.
We had but one life,
Value your friends and family.
Love the life you live,
And live the life you love.

Priyanshi Porwal

Priyanshi Porwal is a 20 year old girl from Indore. An aspiring doctor, she began her medical education recently. Besides the big dream to help mankind, her interest in poetry and painting has always been appreciable. Trying to polish the poet within, she came on the forefront with an ins tagram handle 'Wondertolove_' and has been an active participant in many Poetry competitions and has also managed to secure good positions in them. With the goal of being a doctor she also wishes to pursue the eloquent poetic aspect of herself.

I Wish...

I wish we could meet again,
Under the same sky,
Where we created our love,
Our memories, our everything!
You are now,close,
Very close, but still far away!

I wish,I could hold this time,
Or replay the whole;
But it'll still never be enough,
Hold me tight,
Until the time rewind!

I miss you,
A bit more I used to do
It is the toughest
I used to do
and I am still doing...
To stay away from you,
Scattered me, in all the possible ways!

I'd fight for the days,
When you are not around and see
I am still fighting,
Since you are not around!

Let me be, the dreamy!
Let me be, the lover!
Cause that's what I can do!
Waiting is killing,
And now I'm used to it too!

The words are getting heavier,

I wish I could hold them;
But it tears me apart!

The Void So Loud

Not a single hand to hold on,
Not a single soul to feel warm.
Though you are always around,
But the void is so loud...

Hiding the scars beneath my dreams;
The journey to miles, steps alone.
Though you are always around,
But the void is so loud…

करीब हो तुम

अहसानो का नहीं
एहसासों का गुलाम है ये प्यार,
तलब तुझे पाने की नहीं
तुझ में फना होने की है।

झूठ-सच से परे
जज़्बातों के शहर में,
दिल के सबसे करीब हो तुम!

कभी दुआ में,
तो कभी आंखों की
नमकीन कहानी हो तुम!

अल्फाजों से परे
ख़्वाबों के शहर में
दिल के सबसे करीब हो तुम!

अनकही बाते

कुछ बातें होती है ऐसी,
जो लबों पर आते-आते टूट जाती हैं,
कुछ मन्नतें होती है ऐसी
जो सजा बनते-बनते बिखर जाती हैं!

तुम्हारी महफ़िल में वक्त का पता ही ना चला,
बस वक्त को थामने का मन करता था...
और उस वक्त को भी जो तेरे मेरे बीच
दरमियां ले आता था।

जो भी वजह थी.. शायद बेवजह थी,
यूहीं नहीं मिलना था तेरा मेरा!
ना ही कोई इक्तिफाक था,
ना ही कोई रिश्ता था पुराना!

जुड़ गया था बस तु मुझ में ऐसे,
जैसे मैं भूल ही गया था खुदको,
नशा सा था उन बातों में तेरी...
जिसे साथ में जोड़ा था, उसे ही टूट न था
जाने क्यों मिटना था उसे,
जिसे जीना था सदिया साथ में।

ये मनचला दिल

ये मनचला दिल साथ तेरे...
पर फिकर उसकी लिए करता जाता,
उसका ज़हन हे करता
और फिर सब सहन हे कर जाता,
ये मनचला दिल साथ तेरे...
पर फिकर उसकी लिए करता जाता,
उसकी आंखों में खुद को है ढूंढा करता
और फिर खामोशी से खुद को है बहला जाता, ये मनचला दिल साथ
तेरे...
पर फिकर उसकी लिए करता जाता ।

Neha Chaudhary

This is Neha Chaudhary 'Nivi ', hailing from the holy city of love 'Mathura'. She is a science graduate and a teacher by profession. For her life is journey and loves to meet new people as well as learning new things. Now writing has become the solace of her heart as she finds it as t   he best therapy to pull out vague thoughts and feelings into the words. Dedicated to her life goals, she loves to enjoy every moment of life. She is a Karma believer walking on the life's trail, spreading smiles and collecting tears. She has   worked as a co-author for many anthologies and you can find her writings on IG : @just_a_baat

Letters You Never Wrote

The unsaid words my soul craved to hear,
that would've melted me into tears.
In the cold ambience of my absence,
sentiments of a lone soul,
that you might have inscribed on a blank page,
my numb fingertips are dying to feel.
The breeze of my presence in your solitude,
Brimming the atrium of your heart,
Implying your hands to spill the ink of love,
my freezing veins yearns to soak.
confessions of your dreams and fears.
Glimpse of your desires,
That you never wrote to me,
Now the old wooden box is filled with empty space,
that I pined to treasure with the love letters of yours
antique and forbidden for your modern world,
full of Virtual friends behind the screens,
with alluring reels and digital texts,
The dreams of old heart have fallen
like the dead leaves of Oak.

"Too Scared To Hurt You"

Blinded by your love,
never thought it can go wrong,
signs were scattered all around,
but I was so lost,
in the illusion of the fantasy world,
that you portrayed so well,
dark nights decorated with dying fireflies
I failed to see the dark truth,
Beneath your sugar-coated white lies,
I misinterpreted the statement,
That night, when you said,
"I am too scared to hurt you."
"I never want you to cry because of me."
I consumed all your words as,
empathy for my wounded heart,
so fallen for your enticing promises,
allured in your façade,
I failed to read the decision,
Already made in your mind,
Perhaps failed to heed the warning,
hidden in your words !!!!

"Till Death Do Us Part"

I'ld follow you to the darkest of the dark,
even when doomed is every star.
I've never dreamt of a wonderland,
rainbows or unicorns flying in heaven at par.
You found me when I was a lost cause,
wandering on the dusty shore.
Void of dreams and will to live,
with a cardiac line falling straight thou
scribbled in the crest & trough.
In the numb cadaver you revived the beat.
For my soul to be alive,
your presence is just enough,
warmth of your touch infused in my blood
instils my zeal to be awake.
It's just you that completes me,
Nothing more nothing less,
In the armour of your open arms,
I've found the home for my heart!!
I swear to love you all of my life,
Till my last breath, till death do us part!!

"मैं, तुम और वक़्त हमारा"

एक अरसा हुआ रहती है कुछ कमी सी है अब हर पल में मेरे,
यादों के झरोखों से झाँकते हैं वो लम्हे साथ के तेरे,
लहरें भी मायूस हो लौट जाती हैं किनारे से,
गूँजती नही हैं यहाँ हँसी अब जो तेरी ।
रेत भी हो चली है रेख्ता,
तरस रही है पाने को आहट क़दमों के तेरी ।
ढलती शामें भी अब खामोश सी हैं,
इंतज़ार में सुन ने को फिर से कोई कहानी तेरी ।
सागर का वो किनारा भी पूछता है अब तो,
"कहाँ बिछड़ गये वो यार जो कभी चलते थे हाथ थाम कर ??"
 खाली राहें भी थक गयी हैं अब तो तेरा रास्ता निहार कर ।
चल अब मैं तोड़ू समय की गुल्लक, इक्कट्ठे कर कुछ सिक्के तू भी
फुर्सत के ।
पूरे कर आयें वो किस्से अधूरे, ज़माना हुआ नहीं मिले हम खुल कर ,
चल सजाएँ फिर एक रंगीन शाम इस भागती दुनिया से छुप कर,
तुम ले आना अपनी मुस्कान, बेफ़िक्री में डूबी कुछ बातें नई,
मैं दोहराऊँगी फिर से वही तेरे अल्फ़ाज़ों में लिखी मेरी कहानी ,
खोलेंगे यादों की अलमारी, छेड़ेंगे फिर कोई बात पुरानी,
सागर किनारे सिंदूरी सांझ में, फिर से हम यूं हाथ थाम कर
देखेंगे फिर वो सूरज ढलता, मैं, तुम और वक़्त हमारा ।

"यूँ ही"

कभी यूँ ही कुछ कहे बिना चुप रहना अच्छा लगता है ।
सिन्दूरी होती साँझ में सागर किनारे,
देखना लहरों पर वो सूरज पिघलते,
सुनना सुकून से तेरी ख़ामोशी
बिन बोले तेरी धड़कन से बातें,
तेरे एहसास में बह जाना अच्छा लगता है ।
कभी यूँ ही कुछ कहे बिना चुप रहना अच्छा लगता है ।
रख कर तेरे कांधे पर सर,
ठहर जाती हैं बातें इन अधरों पर,
छोड़ सवाल अन्तर्मन के,
बैचेनी जग की सब बिसरा कर,
तेरी बाहों में खो जाना अच्छा लगता है ।
कभी यूँ ही कुछ कहे बिना चुप रहना अच्छा लगता है ।
गहराती रात के आलम में,
साथ लिए तेरी यादों के साये,
अपनी तन्हाई से वो तेरी बातें,
तेरी यादों मे खो कर यूँ ही,
इस दर्द को सहना अच्छा लगता है ।
कभी यूँ ही कुछ कहे बिना चुप रहना अच्छा लगता है ।

Paramjit Kaur

Paramjit is an introvert. By profession, she is an engineer. Apart from this, she loves to spend time in nature and collect knowledge about the beautiful creations of life. She is very fond of discovering the deep buried secrets of life. So, she likes to read about them. She wants to make a valuable change in society by her contribution in terms of helping the destitute people and endangered animals. She loves to talk to herself.

Instagram Handle @mahworld_

Failures As Learning Lessons

Failures come to test you, not to break you.

Failures give you the opportunity to polish the weak areas of your life, so as to make the best version of yourself you could ever be.

Every failure you encounter, ignites the fire inside you to face challenges with ease.

Failures make you aware of your true potential, which is buried under your deep fear of failing.

God puts failures in your path as learning lessons to make you grow at soul level and beautify your thinking.

Failure seems like darkness in a room, where there is no light. This is what people assume, but there is always a tiny hidden hole in every room through which light could find its path. So, be an optimist and search for that hole in your life's room to fill light into your heart!

The Essence Of Love

Love is blind, I have heard this many times. The day I met you, I fell for you and lost my senses. That day I realized how true it is! Love is really blind!

One-sided love always offers the lover the deadliest slow poison to drink every night alone.

Love has immense magical healing power. It can beat any existing force of the universe while healing the wounds.

The day I met you, I felt a deep connection with you. The day I talked to you, I was overwhelmed with joy. The day I got to know you, I was confused with reality. The day I fought with you, I cried inside. The day I was rude to you, I felt like changing my words. The day I crossed you, I felt something was lost. The day you turned your feet around, I was stuck there. The day you walk   ed out, I was left with nothing.

Success Mantras

Victory comes through suffering only. The more you suffer, the more successful you'll be.

The secrets of successful people are mental toughness, self - belief and self-motivation.

Oh success, why are you upset with me? For years, I have been waiting for you to be mine. Every day I see you going somewhere. Then, why can't you be mine? I am working hard for you, please let this anger go away and come to my side this time. Day and night I ask when will you be mine?

Anything that is earned through struggling a lot, tastes sweeter than sugar candy!

Be thankful to life for lending you in a struggling phase, to shape you into a non-brittle diamond.

If, success is the moon and failure is the earth, then, the struggle is the distance between both.

Yes, I am struggling daily to live life. Yes, I am struggling to overcome the darkness hiding inside me. Yes, I am struggling to control my emotions. Yes, I am struggling to find peace. Yes, I am struggling to fill my heart with joy. Yes, I'm struggling to match the footsteps with life and that is killing me inside!

Perseverance holds the key to end the struggle.

From distance, struggle appears as a mountain but the moment you initiate steps forward towards it. It red uces its size and allows you to climb.

असफलता से सीख

असलता देखकर घबरा मत जाना कभी,
अपने होसले को सदा बूलंद रखना।।
जो आज असंभव नजर आता है,
वो कल बूलंद हौसले से पार हो जाएगा।
असफलता भी सफलता मे तब्दील हो जाएगी।।

हार से डर कर, बीच सफर मत रूक जाना, माना की तुम्हारी
जिंदगी में आज अंधेरा है,
पर कल उजाला भी आऐगा।
एक-एक कर कदम बढ़ाते रहना। रास्ता अपने आप बन जाएगा।
जो आज सपना सा नजर आता है, वो कल तुम्हें अपने आप मिल
जाएगा। परख रही होगी तकददीर तुम्हें वक्त-वक्त पर ,पर हार के
डर से बीच सफर मत रुक जाना कही।

अगर सफल होने का ख्वाब है दिल मे,
तो तू पंख तो फैला, इस जहां को अपनी ताकत दिखला,
चट्टान बनकर डट जा मुश्किलों के राह में,
बस अब तू ना धबरा, जो हँसते है तेरी हार पर   अब तू उन्हें कुछ
करके दिखा,
जो देते है ताना तुझको उनको तू सफल हो कर दिखा।।

प्यार एक एहसास

प्यार एक एहसास है। इसे लफ्जों मे बयान नही किया जा सकता, ये वो एहसास है जिसे सिर्फ महसूस किया जा सकता है। प्यार मे रुह निखर जाती है, चेहरा नूर से भर जाता है, आंखों मे चमक आ जाती है, जिदंगी सुहानी लगने लगती है। आप अपने हमसफर के साथ दुख-सुख बाँटने लगते हो, कुछ अपनी कहते हो और कुछ उनकी सुनते हो, एक दूसरे से ज़िंदगी भर साथ निभाने के वादे करते हो, कुछ ऐसा होता है प्यार का एहसास!

मुझे मोहब्बत मे वफा सिखाकर फिर क्यों किसी और से वफा कर बैठे तुम।
मुझे जीने के रास्ते दिखाकर फिर क्यों किसी और की मंजिल बन बैठे तुम।।
मुझे मुसकूराना सिखाकर फिर क्यों किसी और की मुसकान बन बैठे तुम।
मुझे खुदा से वाकिफ करवाकर फिर क्यों किसी और के खुदा बन बैठे तुम।
मुझे जिदंगी से मिलाकर फिर क्यों किसी और कि जिदगी बन बैठे तुम।
मेरी मोहब्बत पर बेवफाई के इल्जाम लगे है, अब तू ही बता किस अदालत में इंसाफ दिलाऊ इसे।

प्यार में अगर सही इंसान मिल जाए तो जिदंगी आबाद हो जाती है, अगर गलत इंसान से दिल लग जाए तो बरबाद हो जाती है।

Shubham Raman

Shubham Raman is a 26 year old youth who hails from Muzaffarpur, Bihar. He is a Medico currently pursuing his internship. He has been a co -author in various anthologies and has been a runner up of a national level poetry competition. He has been creating poetry since his childhood. He has a keen interest in sports too. He is aspiring to be a surgeon in the near future.

You can contact him via raman.shubham1212@gmail.com
IG @shubham.raman

अनोखा रिश्ता

कुछ अनजाने लोग कब खास हो जाते हैं पता नहीं चलता और हमारे
जीवन का एक अहम हिस्सा बन जाते हैं ।
खून का रिश्ता नहीं होता,
मगर उस से बढ़कर निभा जाते हैं ।

जुबान से नहीं आंखों और चेहरे से समझते हैं हमें ।
भले दूर ही क्यों ना हो कमीने याद बहुत आते हैं ।
पुरानी मस्ती और शरारतों की माला पीरों कर ख्वाबों के बवंडर में उड़ा
ले जाते हैं ।

उनका प्यार जताने का ढंग भी कुछ निराला होता है , जन्मदिन पर बुरी
तरह सूत देना और उदास होने पर मूवी या कहीं बाहर जबरदस्ती ले
चलना या किसी भी लड़की से बात करते देखने पर भाभी - भाभी करके
पूरे समय चिढ़ाना और रातों में भूख लगने पर मैगी खिलाना ।

दोस्त, मित , मित्र , सहचर सब उन्हीं के तो नाम हैं | जिंदगी है तो उनसे
है वरना यह जिंदगी वीरान है ।

' हकीकत '

ख्वाबों को हकीकत बनाकर देखो।
मेहनत को आभूषण बनाकर देखो।
कोई मंजिल दूर नहीं रहेगी तुझसे देख लेना।
बस ईश्वर से पहले मां-बाप को हृदय में बसा कर देखो।
यह धन दौलत यस रह जाएगा इस धरती पर तेरा
अगर कमाना है तो लोगों की दुआ कमा कर देखो।
अगर बहते हैं अश्रु तो बहने दो।

मिट जाते हैं फासले सारे बस एक बार दुश्मन को भी
सच्चे मन से गले लगाकर देखो।
और कहते हैं सब मैं तुमसे प्यार करता हूं
अगर प्यार है तो लबों से नहीं कर्मों से निभा कर देखो।
यह कलयुग का आतंक विलुप्त हो जाएगा देख लेना,
बस धर्म जात ऊंच-नीच का भेदभाव मिटाकर तो देखो।

"आ जाओ लौट कर तुम "

जो कभी मुझे समझते थे,
आज उनकी नासमझी से हैरान हूं ।
लोगों की बातों से नहीं,
बस उनकी खामोशी से परेशान हूं ।
जिनसे दिल की हर एक बातें की थी,
आज उन्हें उन बातों पर,
सवाल और निशान है।
कल जो उनकी आंखें बता देती थी,
क्यों आज उन्हीं की हर बातों से अनजान हूं।
यह दिल रोता है तेरे लिए,
क्या तुम्हें इस पर भी कोई
सवाल और निशान है ।
आ जाओ लौट कर तुम -
आ जाओ लौट कर तुम।।

अधूरी मोहब्बत

तेरे लफ़्ज़ों के इशारे को ना समझ सका,
तेरे दिल के इशारे को ना समझ सका।
इतना प्यार कर बैठा तुझसे,
ना खुद को समझ सका;ना तुझे समझा सका।।

अधूरी रह गई हमारी कहानी, जहाँ मैं ना राजा था, मगर तू थी रानी।
सोचा था मिलोगी तुम कभी ना कभी, चाहे क्यों ना हो कयामत की
शाम ही सही।।

अब तो निकल कर आँखों से यादों में जा बसी हो तुम,
लोग कहते हैं मुझको भुला चुकी हो तुम।
मगर इस दिल की एक ही फरमाइश है,
तु खुश रहे बस यही ख्वाहिश है, बस यही ख्वाहिश है।।

' मासूमियत '

तेरी मासूमियत मुझे कुछ यूं हर कर गई,
नींदें छोड़ो धड़कनों में बसर कर गई,
प्यारी हो तुम, सताती हो तुम,
बिना पास रहे अपनी मौजूदगी दिलाती हो तुम।

माना थोड़ी बच्ची हो अक्ल से थोड़ी कच्ची हो, मगर दिल तेरा इतना
साफ है,
जैसे बरसात की हर बूंदों में तेरा ही आवास है। तेरी मीठी बोली मेरे
कानों में कुछ यूं हर कर जाती है,
जैसे डाली पर बैठी कोयल गाती है।
नौटंकी की सरदार हो तुम,
गुस्से की बौछार हो तुम,
मानो या ना मानो जो भी हो बेमिसाल हो तुम।

Poonam Rathore

Poonam Rathore is her pen name, she loves nature and has a different connection with it. She is a writer and has several writings on Poetizer. For her spreading positivity and teaching lessons of life through her writings is the main goal. Instagram: @_poonam.writes.

प्यार

प्यार छोटा सा लब्ज़ है, जीवन की कहानी है,
हर दिल की प्यास है, आंखो का पानी है,
सपनों के गांव में ख्वाहिशों के मेले हैं,
तारों की छांव में चाहतों के डेरे हैं,
दिलों पे दस्तक इसकी निशानी है,
प्यार छोटा सा लब्ज़ जीवन की कहानी है|

प्यारी सी कशिश है, खुबसूरत सा एहसास है,
अंजाने दिलो में, पहचाना सा विश्वास है,
मिटाने से भी जो न मिटे वो अमिट निशानी है,
प्यार छोटा सा लब्ज़ है जीवन की कहानी है|

जिंदगी की पहली धड़कन है ये,
आखिरी सांस की तड़पन है ये
इसके बिना क्या जिंदगानी है,
प्यार छोटा सा लब्ज़ है जीवन की कहानी है|

हर दिल की प्यास है,
आंखों का पानी है|

प्रेम

दिल के आईने में एक तस्वीर उभरने दो,
बांधो मत बंधन में इसे चाहत का रंग भरने दो,
मूक है इसकी भाषा एक सुखद एहसास है,
स्वाति नक्षत्र की बूंद है, चकोर की अमिट प्यास है,
इठलाती नदी के आंचल से ये, मधुमास गुजरने दो,
बांधो मत बंधन में इसे, चाहत का रंग भरने दो।

खनकती चूडियो में इसका संगीत है,
झनकती पायल में इसका गीत है,
दबे पाव आकर कहती है,
हवा ये तेरा मनमीत है,
इंद्रधनुष के रंगो से चेहरे को निखरने दो,
बांधो मत बंधन में इसे, चाहत के रंग भरने दो।

इसमें विरह की तड़प है, तो मिलने को आश भी है,
प्रेम का आशय तो, इक दूजे मे विश्वास है,
ख्वाबो के पंख ले परवान भरने दो,
बांधो मत बंधन में इसे, चाहत का रंग भरने दो,
प्रेयसी का श्रृंगार है, ये मां की ममता का गीत है,
सतत है, निरंतर है,
होती सदा इसकी जीत हैं,
मेरे इस गीत को प्यार से सवरने दो,
दिल के आईने में इक तस्वीर उभरने दो,
बांधो मत बंधन में इसे, चाहत का रंग भरने दो।

त्याग

त्याग जीवन की अमिट निशानी है,
प्रेम से जुड़ी इसकी कहानी है,
बुद्ध ने राजसी जीवन दिया था त्याग,
पाने को ज्ञान ले लिया था बैराग,
बन के भिक्षुक दिया था उपदेश,
भूल नही सकते उनका उद्देश्य,
त्याग के बिना देशभक्ति असंभव है,
निज स्वार्थ को त्याग के ही, जन सेवा संभव है,
त्यागा न होता जो जीवन का सुकून,
कैसे मिलती आजादी जो त्याग का होता न जुनून,
मां का प्यार है त्याग की असीम गहराई,
उसके दिल से जुड़ी होती है सफलता की ऊंचाई,
उसके त्याग की नींव से मजबूत होते हैं इरादे,
अपनी ख्वाहिशों को त्याग पूरे करती है वादे,
त्याग में छिपी समर्पण की कहानी है,
त्याग जीवन की अमिट निशानी है|

असफलता

दृढ़ निश्चय करके तुम आगे बढ़ते जाना,
मिले अगर असफलता तुमको तो बिल्कुल मत घबराना,
रखना नजर लक्ष्य पे अपनी धुंधली न हो मंजिल,
विश्वास अटूट हो अपने ऊपर कितनी भी हो मुश्किल,
जो कमी थी लक्ष्य पाने में उसे फिर से मत दोहराना,
मिले अगर असफलता तो बिल्कुल मत घबराना।
कितनी बार असफल हुए लोगो ने तब मंजिल पाई है,
मजबूत हौसला रखके दिल में ख़ुद अपनी राह बनाई है,
आलोचनाओं के घिरे हों बादल करनी क्या परवाह,
असफलताओं में राह तलाश ले रखना ऐसी चाह,
न निराशा मन में हो न उत्साह में जरा आए कमी,
नजरों में सिर्फ लक्ष्य हो अपना आंखो में न हो नमी,
कर प्रयास निरंतर चलना थकने का तुम नाम न लेना,
मिलेगी तुझको तेरी मंजिल, असफलता से निराश न होना।
असफलता को समझ के सीढ़ी उपर तुम चढ़ते जाना,
मिले अगर असफलता तुमको तो बिल्कुल मत घबराना
दृढ़ निश्चय करके तुम आगे बढते जाना।

सफलता

आंखो में सूरज के उजाले ,चांद तारों पे नजर रखते है,
दिखा दो इस जमाने को हम भी, बेहतर बनने का हुनर रखते है|
जुगनुओं की रोशनी में रातों का सफर,
करने का हौसला रखते है,
हम समंदर की तरह सह कर,
तूफानों में लहरों को झेला करते हैं।
हम कठिनाइयां कितनी भी हों राहों में,
बस मंजिल पे नजर रखते है,
आंखो में सूरज के उजाले चांद तारों पे नजर रखते है|
परवाह नहीं करते है हम काफिलों की,
बस दिल में जुनून होता है, आसमां पे रहती है,
अपनी ये नजर संग में तूफानों का हुजूम होता है,
हम खुद को कैद नही करते बंदिशों में,
बस टूटे न सपने किसी के दुआओं में असर रखते है,
आंखों में सूरज के उजाले और चांद तारों पे नजर रखते हैं|

Navneet Singh Charan

Navneet, an engineer by profession and writer by passion. He started writing in 2018. He loves to write about love, history, freedom fighters, struggle of today's society like politics, rape cases etc.

Connect with him on various platforms

Instagram — charan_poetry

Twitter- Navneet19singh

Visit — https://charan19poetry.blogspot.com/?m=0

एक मुलाक़ात ऐसी भी ।

बेठा हूँ रात के सन्नाटे में ,
ओर मीठी हवा चल रही है ।।

सर हल्का भारी सा लग रहा है
आँखे भरी भरी सी लग रही है,
महसूस करने की कोशिश करी मेने ,
दिल बोला , शायद किसी की कमी खल रही है।।

मन हुआ उससे बात करने का,
मेने आँखे बन्द कर ली ...!!

मेने आँखे बंद कर ली
अब सामने वो खड़ी है,
पुछा मेने उससे
क्या तुम्हें भी मेरी कमी खल रही है...

शांत खड़ी है वो एकदम
क्योंकि नज़रें मुझसे मिल रही है,
शायद जान गयी है वो
के ग़लती तो उसने करी है ।।

मुस्कुराया में और बोला उससे
देखो ये दुनिया कितनी बुरी है,
और ग़लती का क्या है
ग़लती तो खुदा ने भी बहुत करी है ।।

फिर से मिली नज़रें और बोली वो
हा ग़लती तो मेने करी है,

हो सके तो माफ़ कर और आगे बढ़
आँखे खोल के देख , ज़िंदगी अभी पुरी पड़ी है ।।

बेठा हूँ रात के सन्नाटे में ,
ओर मीठी हवा चल रही है ।।

उस पीड़ा के दौर के हम किरदार थे !

सुना था

के आयी थी कोई बीमारी एसी
के गाँव के गाँव ख़ाली हो गये थे ,
रोए थे पशु पक्षी भी
लोगों के पूरे परिवार ख़ाली हो गए थे ...

अजीब लगता था सुन के
भला एसे भी रोग हो सकते है क्या ,
अरे कुछ 2-4 मरे होंगे
एसे कोई परिवार खो सकते है क्या ...

पर

देखा एक अनोखा तांडव हमने
कुछ को ज़मीर बेचते कुछ को भगवान बनते देखा है ,
छीना कई परिवारों को इसने
पर कई हज़ारों को सोनू सूद और कुमार विश्वास बनते देखा है ...

फिर कोई सुनेगा कहानिया हमसे
बेटा सन्नाटे में चीख़ते कई मझदार थे ,
साँसो की कालाबाज़ारी हुई
ज़मीर के कई सौदेबाज हुए ...

सरकारों और कारोबारियों ने बड़ी ज़िल्लत ढहायी थी ,
शायद इन कमभक्तो ने अपने कफ़न में जेबें लगवायी थी ...

शायद कहीं ना कहीं
हम ख़ुद ही इस सब के ज़िम्मेदार थे ,
जैसी बन पड़ी सम्भाली हमने
उस पीड़ा के दौर के हम ख़ुद किरदार थे ...

कुछ भी करो पर अब बचा लो , चाहे पूरा संविधान बदल डालो ।।

कुछ भी करो पर अब बचा लो ,
चाहे पूरा संविधान बदल डालो ।।

ओर किसका है अब इंतज़ार
सारी हदें हो चुकी है पार,
कुछ बाक़ी नहि बचा है
इंसानियत भी जलके हो चुकी है राख ।।

अब वक़्त नहीं है सोचने का
के क्यू ये सब कर जाते है,
अपनी हवस बुझाने को
आख़िर इतना केसे गिर जाते है।।

अब बहुत हुआ समझना भुझाना
सीधा सीधा सुलझाना होगा ,
एक दो को बीच चोराहे
जीते जी जलाना होगा ।।

अब ओर नहीं सहा जाता
अब ओर नहीं देखा जाता ,
अब कुछ तो करना होगा
देश के बहार बाद में लड़ लेंगे
पहले भीतर भारत बचाना होगा ।।

ये हर दिन देश की बेटि नहीं
ख़ुद भारत माँ चीख़ रही है,
कुछ भी करो पर अब बचालो

नए क़ानून बनाओ
धारा लगाओ
ओर ज़रूरत पड़ने पर
चाहे पूरा संविधान बदल डालो !!

कुछ भी करो पर अब बचा लो
चाहे पूरा संविधान बदल डालो...

Pramesh Kumar

Pramesh Kumar is a writer who writes from his core. He is a budding and blooming personality in the literary world. He always tries his best to put his head and heart on paper with his pen. He pours down an ocean of thoughts in a flow of just a few words. He always gives his readers a direct way to his thoughts and life experience. His minute observation of worldly things and aspects gives a charm in his writing. After all, he is a lover of nature and humanity.

He rightly says about his writing, "Every word of my writing is not only a combination of letters but my heartbeat which gives life to my literary arts".

उम्मीद की किरण

घुट-घुट कर ऐ जीने वालों, गम के आंसू पीने वालों,
कुछ बादल के छँट जाने से, सावन नहीं मरा करता है,
जीवन तो काँटों के सेज पे जैसे कोई गुलाब कली,
और टूटना उसका जैसे हवा में चंदन गंध भीनी|

खुद को बेबस करने वालों,अपने को हीन समझने वालों,
एक दर्पण के टूट जाने से तस्वीर नहीं टूटा करती है,
कुछ चाहत छूट गयी तो क्या,कुछ सपने टूट गए तो क्या,
एक पुष्प के टूट जाने से उपवन नहीं टूटा करता है|

खुद को लघु समझने वालों,अपने को दुखी बताने वालों,
कुछ पत्तो के झड़ जाने से,बसंत नहीं रोया करता है,
अपने छूट गए तो क्या,कुछ हँसकर रूठ गए तो क्या
कुछ अपनों के खो जाने से जीवन नहीं खोया करते हैं|

खोता कुछ भी नहीं यहाँ पर, केवल शक्ल बदलती नियति,
एक सिक्के के सुख-दुख दो पहलू, सदैव अपनी धुरी पर फिरते
घोर क्लेश में जीने वालों, उम्मीद से मुँह को मोड़ने वालों,
इक रोज़ अमावास आ जाने से,सूरज नहीं छिपा करता है|

सैकड़ो बार नियति यह बदली,लाखों बार उम्मीदें टूटी,
अपनी उम्र गवाने वालों, दुःख की उम्र बढ़ाने वालों,
केवल आँखों के सो जाने से,सपनें नहीं सोया करते हैं,
बस एक दिन दुःख के आ जाने से वीर नहीं रोया करते है|

है क़सम हमें इस मिट्टी की!

है क़सम हमें इस मिट्टी की हम देश का क़र्ज़ चुकाएंगे,
जब-जब वतन की बात आये हम अपना लहू बहाएंगे,
दे देंगे प्राण बलिदान स्वरूप निरर्थक न जग से जायेंगे;
है क़सम हमें इस मिट्टी की हम देश का क़र्ज़ चुकाएंगे।

है देश-प्रेम दिल में सबके, अब अन्य न कोई प्रेम रहा,
मिली मातृभूमि भारत जैसी ऐसा अपना सौभाग्य रहा;
जब-जब वतन पर आक्रान्त का होगा कोई प्रहार कभी,
तप,त्याग,युद्ध सब कुछ करके हम देश की आन बचाएंगे ,
है क़सम हमें इस मिट्टी की हम देश का क़र्ज़ चुकाएंगे।

हो देश प्रेम सबसे ऊपर, हो मातृभूमि सबके मन पर,
ऐसी भारत की शान बढ़े जग में भारत का मान बढ़े,
लेते हैं प्रण के जीते जी हम कभी न पीठ दिखाएंगे,
है क़सम हमें इस मिट्टी की हम देश का क़र्ज़ चुकाएंगे।

जब वतन पर कोई आंच आये, तो चारों भाई साथ आयें,
लेते हैं प्रण के प्राण त्याग कर देश का मान बचाएंगे,
है क़सम हमें इस मिट्टी की हम देश का क़र्ज़ चुकाएंगे।

जब-जब वतन की बात आये हम अपना लहू बहाएंगे
है क़सम हमें इस मिट्टी की हम देश का क़र्ज़ चुकाएंगे।

ऐ काश!

ऐ काश ! के हमारी मुलाक़ात ही न हुई होती,

कम से कम ये दिल तन्हा रोता तो नहीं,

ऐ काश ! हमने दिल तुम्हें दिया ही न होता,

कम से कम ये दुखता तो नहीं|

ऐ काश ! के हम तुमसे इतनी मोहब्बत ही न करते,

कम से कम दिल-ए-सुकून गवाते तो नहीं,

ऐ काश ! के तेरे मोहब्बत में हम डूबे ही न होते,

कम से कम खुद को तो सम्हाल पाते|

ऐ काश ! के तुमसे इतनी गुफ़्तगू ही न होती,

कम से कम आज ख़ामोश तो न रहते,

ऐ काश ! ताउम्र साथ रहने का ख्वाब ही न देखा होता,

कम से कम कोई दूसरा ख़्वाब देखने से डरते तो नहीं|

मैं भी तुम्हारे लिए उतना ही ख़ास हूँ जितना तुम मेरे लिए,

ऐ काश ! के सोचा ही न होता कम से कम आज लाचार तो न होता,

ऐ काश ! तुमने भी मुझसे उतना ही प्यार किया होता,

जितने की मैंने तुमसे कम से कम आज तन्हा तो न होता|

जो हुआ सो हुआ,

ऐ काश ! के हम इतने दूर ही न हुए होते,

ऐ काश ! के हमारे रस्ते ही न अलग हुए होते,

ऐ काश ! के हम मिल जाते,

ऐ खुदा तेरा क्या चला जाता अगर हम दो एक हो जाते ?

ऐ काश...!

बस कर ऐ ज़िन्दगी!

बस कर ऐ ज़िंदगी,अब थक चूका हूँ मैं,
तेरे इम्तहान के आगे,अब झुक चुका हूँ मैं,
खुशियाँ इतनी लीं और ग़म इतने दिए
के तेरे इस खेल को अब समझ चुका हूँ मैं|

तेरी दी हुयी तकलीफ़ों से तकलीफ़ नहीं मुझे,
बस इस सिलसिले के ख़त्म होनें का डर लगा रहता है,
मेरे खुशियों में मेरे साथ होते हैं सब पर,
तकलीफ़ में तलाशता हूँ,के कौन मेरे साथ होता है|

इस क़दर गुज़री है मेरी ज़िंदगी तकलीफ़ों के किनारे,
के हर नई सुबह मेरा वही हाल रहता है,
और दुनियाँ पूछती है मेरी मंज़िल मुझ से,
कह दे उन्हें के अब हार चुका हूँ मैं|

तेरे हर रोज़ के इम्तहान की फ़िकर नहीं मुझे,
न तेरी तूफानी संघर्षों से डर लगता है,
लोगों ने कुछ ऐसे बदली है फितरत अपनी के,
अपनों में छिपे गैरों से घबराता हूँ|

अब तो मौत भी रास्ता देखती है मेरा पीछे मुड़कर,
कह दे उसके बस...करीब पहुँच चुका हूँ मैं,
बस कर ऐ ज़िंदगी अब थक चूका हूँ मैं,
तेरे इम्तहान के आगे अब झुक चुका हूँ मैं |

Flairs and Glairs, a platform by a student for   the students. We are esteemed youth struggling to carve out our path for our future and we follow a basic mindset Since everyone is not born with all   -round skills. Joining hands with people who are born to execute it with perfection is the best way to evol   ve. Self -Evolution is the need of the hour but, evolving as a community is what we strive for. The initiative as kickstarted by, Founder - Mr. Shubham Shah with the motive to utilize the skillset and talent of writing has now a team of 10+ people who are ac   tively participating into newer forms of learning and discovering talents among youngsters.   We Provide platform and services like Publishing opportunities, Open mics, Workshops, Hands -on training. Operating with Brand Name of Flairs and Glairs   (Publication House), we offer the chance of elevating a passionate writer to an esteemed author   With Brand name Teekhe Zasbaaat. We bring to you an opportunity to get accustomed with the Public Speaking and Presenting of Thoughts along with regular challen ges to brush up your inking spirit.   The newest initiative to extend our services we introduced in a new writing Platform- The Glittering Fables and Ink Over Tears.

We Choose to Fly Like A Falcon than to be

a Leg Pulling Crab.

To Know More: Infoline – 7781900870
Mail Us At-
flairsandglairs@gmail.com / info@flairsandglairs.in
Or Visit is at
www.flairsandglairs.com / www.flairsandglairs.in
Social Handles- @flairsandglairs @teekhezasbaaat